S0-BOG-875

# ER DOC TO MISTLETOE BRIDE

—

## LOUISA GEORGE

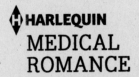

PAPL
DISCARDED

**HARLEQUIN**

MEDICAL
ROMANCE

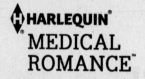

# HARLEQUIN®
## MEDICAL
## ROMANCE™

Recycling programs
for this product may
not exist in your area.

ISBN-13: 978-1-335-40896-9

ER Doc to Mistletoe Bride

Copyright © 2021 by Louisa George

This edition published by arrangement with Harlequin Books S.A.

For questions and comments about the quality of this book, please contact us at CustomerService@Harlequin.com.

Harlequin Enterprises ULC
22 Adelaide St. West, 40th Floor
Toronto, Ontario M5H 4E3, Canada
www.Harlequin.com

**Printed in U.S.A.**

Award-winning author **Louisa George** has been an avid reader her whole life. In between chapters she's managed to train as a nurse, marry her doctor hero and have two sons. Now she writes chapters of her own in the medical romance, contemporary romance and women's fiction genres. Louisa's books have been nominated for the coveted RITA® Award and the New Zealand Koru Award, and have been translated into twelve languages. She lives in Auckland, New Zealand.

### Books by Louisa George

**Harlequin Medical Romance**

***Royal Christmas at Seattle General***
*The Princess's Christmas Baby*

***SOS Docs***
*Saved by Their One-Night Baby*

***The Ultimate Christmas Gift***
*The Nurse's Special Delivery*

***The Hollywood Hills Clinic***
*Tempted by Hollywood's Top Doc*

*Tempted by Her Italian Surgeon*
*Reunited by Their Secret Son*
*A Nurse to Heal His Heart*
*A Puppy and a Christmas Proposal*
*Nurse's One-Night Baby Surprise*

Visit the Author Profile page
at Harlequin.com for more titles.

To the Waipu Ocean Diving Sistahs…
thank you for teaching this old dog

a) amazing new tricks, and

b) that, whatever I'm doing, I must always finish in style ;-)

This book wouldn't exist without you. Thanks for the brainstorming, the love and the laughter xxx

**Praise for
Louisa George**

"A single dad, an unexpected pregnancy, secret crush, friends to lovers, Louisa George combines so many of my favourite tropes in her latest outing to Oakdale…. [T]his series is right up there with Sarah Morgan['s] medical romances…and it's no secret how much I love those."
—*Goodreads* on *Nurse's One-Night Baby Surprise*

# CHAPTER ONE

As a successful ER doctor who'd won scores of grants and awards, Rachel Tait prided herself on never making mistakes in her job. Unfortunately, she couldn't be quite so glib about her personal life.

She stared out of the taxi at the snowy landscape of Sainte Colette unfolding before her: the laughing children throwing snowballs, the pack of huskies pulling a sled carrying a clearly besotted couple, the snow-covered mountains and the blackest night sky lit with thousands of stars, the cute Swiss-style chalets and the twinkling lights strewn across the resort's reception façade and threaded through tree branches.

It looked like something out of a movie set.

And she had to admit it was also looking very much like another personal mistake she'd spend the next four months regretting.

Why had she chosen somewhere so very *Christmassy* to spend Christmas?

Why hadn't she chosen Australia, or the Maldives…? Or somewhere where they didn't cel-

ebrate Christmas at all? Surely that would have
been a better idea than this?

Lesson learnt. Taking the first job offered to
her just so that she could escape Leeds General
Hospital hadn't been her finest decision-making
moment.

Objectively, she could see Sainte Colette was enchanting. And bitterly cold. Perhaps, she laughed
to herself, she could actually *become* the Ice Queen
she'd so often been accused of being. Hopefully,
the cold would be contagious and she'd be able to
freeze her heart, too, and prevent it from ever getting hurt again.

She shook herself. She'd come here to forget,
not to remember.

After paying the driver she looped her handbag
across her body, hefted one hold-all under one
arm, hauled another up on to her left shoulder,
gripped the wheelie-suitcase handle, then wondered what to do with the skis...

She'd come here to forget, but the memories
still hit her with force, and all she could see was
the long stretch of aisle ahead of her. Still felt the
kick in her heart.

She swallowed.

Still saw the apologetic look on the vicar's face
as she walked towards him...the embarrassed
best man...

*'Puis je vous aider avec vos bagages?'*

What to do with the skis? She put the bags back

down on the icy ground and looked for a ski rack she could leave them in while she checked in. There. To the right of the entrance. She left her bags while she stashed her skis, then retraced her steps for her luggage. Hefted two bags on to her shoulders and dipped to grasp the suitcase handle. She felt like a packhorse.

'*Vos bagages, mademoiselle?*'

The grip of her father's hand on her arm as the truth had finally dawned…made so much worse because it had taken a lot of organising for her parents to attend such an event together. Humiliation instead of joy on what should have been the happiest day of her life….

And now she was here. To forget.

It was proving to be a lot harder than she'd thought.

'Ahem. *Puis je vous aider?*'

She was vaguely aware of a deeply resonant voice saying something in French and looked up into soft, dark-brown eyes. A man, behind the reception desk, was staring at her as if she had two heads. What had he said? *Can I help you?* 'Oh. Right. Check-in. Yes.'

The man nodded. '*Bonsoir, mademoiselle. Bienvenue à Sainte Colette.*'

She was in France, she needed to practise her language skills. Okay. Yes. She'd rehearsed this. What was it? *I'd like the keys to my bedroom.* She cleared her throat and said, rather more slowly than she'd have liked, *'Oui. Bonsoir. Je... Je souhaiterais récupérer les clés de ma chambre.'*

'Of course.' He understood! She'd clearly nailed it. A smile hovered around the corners of his mouth. The dark eyes shifted down to the screen. 'Please, just one moment, Miss…?'

Rachel leaned against the reception counter. 'Dr. *Docteur.*'

'I beg your pardon. Dr…?' He wasn't wearing a name badge but, despite the smile, had that air of authority that, in her experience, only existed in high-end establishments such as the Sainte Colette ski resort.

Handsome, in a super-clichéd kind of way. All nice eyes and swept-back dark hair. Stubbled jaw. Sexy-as-hell accent that tugged at her gut.

Not that she was noticing men these days, or ever again. One broken heart per lifetime was quite enough. She met his arrogant air with one of her own and tried to remember what *I am called* was in French. 'Er… *Je m'appelle* Dr Rachel Tait.'

What had she done with the email the ski resort owner had sent her with her orientation instructions? She dug into her handbag for her phone. 'I'm here… *J'ai…*'

She'd practised this, too, but the three-hour journey winding up into the mountains had made her nauseous and sleepy. Speaking a foreign language was a stretch right now.

The man smiled at her, probably out of pity for

her woeful accent. 'I speak English if that would be easier.'

*Thank God.* It dawned on her that the last three things he'd said had been in English and she hadn't even noticed. She'd been thinking about being jilted at the altar. Why had she dragged her depressing past along with her? It was weighing heavier on her than the three bags plus skis. She was supposed to be healing, not moping.

She looked at the man and nodded. 'Much easier. Yes. Thank you. Good.'

'Welcome to Sainte Colette.' He handed her a swipe card in a little cardboard holder. 'Here is the key to your chalet. Number twelve. Behind this building, round the corner to the left. I will call Frederik to assist you.'

Tempting. In her haste to leave the country she hadn't given much thought to what she'd need for four months in the French Alps, so she'd pretty much packed the entire contents of her wardrobe. Juggling three bags and skis had been difficult to say the least.

And the truth was, she desperately wanted someone to help her, just once in her life, and to be able to drop the *I'm fine* pretence she'd been putting on since that hot July day...since as long as she could remember, in fact. Her heart ached to say yes to his offer, but she didn't have the energy to make niceties with someone she didn't know, and she firmly believed that if she said she was fine enough times then she would start to believe it. 'No need. I'm fine.'

The man looked surprised by her rejection. 'But—'

'I can manage, thank you,' she cut him off as weariness seeped into her bones. The bag on her left shoulder was pinching the skin on her neck. The other holdall was balanced between her knees and the reception-counter strut. She wasn't sure she could hold it in that position for much longer. Plus, she needed to pee.

'We have welcome drinks in the bar—'

'No. I've been travelling for what feels like days. I'm going straight to bed.' Welcome drinks? Did he think she was a guest? She hated small talk and couldn't think of anything worse than enforced mixing and mingling. All she wanted was to soak in the spa bath she'd been promised in the room spec, have an early night and be fresh for her first day tomorrow. Then she could meet, and hopefully impress, her new boss and get on with her job.

The man with no name badge nodded. 'I'd like to—'

'No.' She held up her hand and enunciated a little more slowly. Even though his spoken English was impeccable, maybe he had trouble understanding it? 'Thank you. I can manage my bags.'

More surprise flickered across his eyes as he appraised her, then he gave one of those shrugs that told her he didn't much care. And she realised, close-up, just how gorgeous he was.

His eyes met hers and she saw gold in the brown. A tenacious strength. They really were quite alluring. He had a presence of calm control...quite the opposite of how she felt right now, being scrutinised by him.

His reply was as slow as her words had been. 'As. You. Wish. Dr Tait.'

'Good.' She bent to allow the heavy holdall balancing on her knees to slide to the floor as she signed the registration forms he'd pushed across the desk. 'Do you have milk?'

'Milk?' He frowned.

'In the chalets. For tea.'

A hoity eyebrow rose. 'Of course. In the fridge.'

'Not the long-life stuff, it makes tea taste horrible. Proper milk? Low fat, if possible.'

A sharp nod. 'I will have some brought to your chalet.'

'Please ask them to knock and leave it outside. I don't want to be disturbed.' Also known as, expecting to be shoulder deep in a deliciously warm bubble bath. 'Oh. And can you contact Matthieu LeFevre and tell him the new resort doctor has arrived? I'm expecting to meet him at eight a.m. sharp tomorrow. I'll need a tour of the facilities.'

She turned and scanned her bags. What else did she need? Anything?

Oh, she hated starting somewhere new. She

liked to be in control, to be confident of her sur-
roundings and space. She didn't like surprises or
uncertainty. No. She couldn't think of anything
else.

She nodded to the man, ignoring the flicker
of attraction prickling over her skin as he gave
a curt nod in return, shifted the bag on her left
shoulder to stop the neck-pinch and went to retrieve her skis. Determined not to make any more
mistakes before the four months were through.

Matthieu watched the new doctor disappear into
the darkness outside and shook his head. Truthfully, he was lost for words and that didn't happen very often.

The automatic glass doors swished open again
and he saw the lone figure heft her bags on to
her shoulders and simultaneously drop a ski, the
slump of her back as she bent down, overbur-
dened with bags, to pick the ski up, only to have
the holdall on her left shoulder drop to the ground.
Watched as Frederik ran to help and saw the hand
she raised to stop him.

What the hell? There was independence and
then there was stubbornness. Matt dashed outside. 'Dr Tait, please let us help.'

'I'll just leave the skis here.' She brushed a
wisp of her dark-auburn bobbed hair back from
her flushed face as she propped the skis back
against the rack. 'I'll pop back for them later.'

'I can—'

'Please.' Her grey eyes grew wide and she shook her head vehemently. 'I can manage.'

He froze and caught her gaze. She meant it. She absolutely didn't want help or conversation or company. Which was an issue in his resort, with a culture that focused on open, positive and, above all, friendly communication. But, given the strained look on her face, he doubted she'd want to hear that right now.

'As you wish.' Sighing, Matt went back inside and called the hotel bar. 'Louis? Matt here. Cancel the welcome drinks for the new doctor. Sorry for all the trouble you went to.'

'Aaargh. Don't tell me he's not coming?' A frustrated sigh that matched Matt's own. Louis was the resort events co-ordinator, bar manager and Matt's number two in command, and equally committed to Sainte Colette being a success. He was also Matt's best friend of about thirty-two of his thirty-four years. 'What are we going to do? We can't run a place this size and not have a medic.'

'Oh, *she's* here all right. She just doesn't want drinks. Or a welcome, as far as I can see.'

'Well, she's here, that's something. We can do the drinks another time.' His friend's voice relaxed. 'What's she like?'

*Difficult* sprang to mind. Frosty. And also beautiful. She'd certainly made an impression. 'I'm wondering whether I should have interviewed her personally instead of letting the agency deal with it, but I was juggling a few things at the time. I'm not sure how she's going to cope with the clients we have here.'

'She's forgotten to pack her kid gloves, right?'

'They pay enough to be treated well. And they expect it.' His heart sank as he thought about her easy dismissal of him and his staff, her offhand manner and invisible but palpable keep-out sign on her forehead. Rich guests had very particular demands and needs. Sometimes, outrageously so—which was something he tried hard not to encourage and didn't pander to, if possible. But, even so, they did deserve civility. 'I'm going to have to talk to her about it first thing tomorrow. We can't have her upsetting people. Trust me, I am not looking forward to having that conversation.'

'Tough love, right?'

'Something like that.' And just like that Matt was thrown back to the last time he'd had to exercise tough love. But it hadn't been with a client or a colleague, it had been with his mother. His gut clenched at the memories and how spectacularly he'd failed.

'Give her a chance, Mattie. She might settle in okay.'

'And she might not. I can't take that risk. Best nip it in the bud at the beginning. I'm going to have to say something.' No matter how much he didn't want to.

'Good luck with that.' Louis laughed. But then he hadn't met the formidable Dr Tait. 'And I meant, what's she *like*, like? Hot?'

'Cold.' But he paused as he remembered the fleeting wistfulness in her large grey eyes when he'd offered help for her bags. And how quickly that wistfulness had been erased. The no-nonsense auburn bobbed hairstyle that framed a pretty face. The determined, fixed jaw.

He'd also noticed the sensuous mouth and form-fitting clothes wrapped around a very attractive body.

And, call him a pushover, but he kept going back to that micro-flicker of vulnerability before she'd slammed the shutters down. He'd been instantly intrigued.

But after tomorrow's difficult conversation with her, any lingering, inconvenient attraction to her would no doubt be extinguished.

*Aargh...* He scrubbed his hand across his head as more frustration rattled through him... *What the hell*? He hated to see someone struggle. He ended the chat with Louis, waited until Zoe, their usual evening receptionist, returned from her break, then he tugged on his gloves and went outside to deliver her skis to her chalet.

Whether she wanted him to or not.

# CHAPTER TWO

THE FIRST THING Rachel noticed when she opened the heavy curtains the next morning was the vista of deep, indigo-blue lake and vertiginous snowy mountains that her bedroom window looked out on to. It was picture-postcard beautiful and made her heart sigh after a lifetime of living in a city. Breathtaking didn't go far enough—it was simply stunning.

The second thing she noticed was the silence.

She couldn't remember the last time she'd heard...well, nothing. The ER department was never quiet; there were always patients, monitors, chatter. Her little Leeds apartment gave on to a main road—all the better for quick and easy access to work—and between traffic sounds, footfall and birdsong there was always noise. To hear nothing at all was disorienting to say the least. Stillness was foreign to her because, even though her body and environment might be still, her brain never was. There was always some challenge to work out: a difficult fracture, a strange illness, an elusive diagnosis. She liked solving problems.

And she loved this cosy chalet. A one-bed-roomed A-frame house hewn out of pale wood. Plaid sofas in the living area and a little dining space with table and two chairs, a roomy bedroom with a comfortable mattress and pillows and the crispest linens, fresh flowers in a vase on the wood table. Scandinavian-inspired decor with everything she could need, including fresh milk and a place for her boots and skis by the front door.

Skis that had been left by an unknown deliverer, although she would have bet money it had been the insufferably over-helpful man from reception last night.

She remembered his soulful dark eyes and the disappointment that had flickered in them when she'd refused his help. No matter. One thing Rachel Tait did not need was a kind man's help. Although…the smile had been warm and friendly and she didn't mind admitting he'd been great eye candy.

And very off limits.

Relationships with colleagues were definitely not going to happen again. She knew that road led straight to heartache. She could look, but absolutely not touch.

She stretched and inhaled the fresh air, feeling a lot more positive than when she'd arrived. Today was the first day in her new job. A new challenge. The job she'd taken because…

She slammed those thoughts back and hurried

to shower, dress quickly in lots of layers and head over to the restaurant for breakfast.

She hadn't really noticed the hotel lobby when she'd been here last night but, along with everything she'd learned so far about Sainte Colette, there'd been no lack of attention to detail when it came to decor and atmosphere. It was modern and airy, but inviting with opulent touches: thick faux-fur throws over deep, inviting couches, a massive, crackling open fire, freshly baked cookies that infused the air with a sweet cinnamon scent. Swathes of tinsel hung from wooden rafters. Fairy lights twinkled in rivulets down slate walls. So far, so Christmassy, although no tree.

She was standing open-mouthed, staring at the extravagant glittering chandelier hanging in the centre of the foyer when she heard a voice behind her.

'Dr Tait. Good morning.' The man from last night. Yesterday, he'd been dressed in a pale blue polo shirt with the resort logo on it, but today he wore a slim-fitting navy-blue padded jacket over a cream merino base layer and narrow-legged black ski pants. He was also not behind the desk, but walking towards her. 'I hope you slept well?'

'Not really, but then I never do the first night in a new place.' How had she not noticed how tall he was? Or how strikingly good looking? *Look, don't touch.* 'Was it you who left my skis outside my chalet?'

He nodded. 'It was.'

As she'd guessed. Insufferably helpful.

And even though she'd been irked because he hadn't done as she'd asked, it had been a kind thing to do. 'Okay. Well, thank you for that.' But now she felt beholden to him, too. She rummaged in her bag for some cash and thrust it at him. 'Okay. Well, thank you.'

He frowned, but didn't take the coins. 'For what?'

'It's a tip.' Was he new? Or did they not tip in France? She thrust them at him again. 'For helping me.'

'Really. No need.' He blinked. 'I'm—'

'I insist,' she interjected and put the money into his hand. But maybe they didn't tip. Oh, dear. Was that insulting? In some cultures it was. He looked so bemused she changed the subject. 'Can you tell me where the restaurant is, please?'

'This way.' Still holding the coins, he walked her across the tiled floor to the Montagne room and pulled out a plush chair for her to sit facing a huge picture window with the same view as her bedroom. The table was set for two people with steaming pots of, she imagined, coffee or hot chocolate.

'Thank you.' She sat down and poured delicious-smelling coffee into a cup. 'Now, could you find um…?' She took out her phone to check the name. 'Matthieu LeFevre? I need to speak to him.'

'The boss? Sure.' But instead of turning away to go find the owner of Sainte Colette resort, he slid into the chair opposite and put the coins on the table.

Rachel sat back, shocked. 'Excuse me. What are you doing?'

'I am Matthieu LeFevre.' With a smug self-satisfied smile, he stuck out his hand. 'Good to be properly introduced at last, Dr Tait.'

No! It couldn't be. This man owned Sainte Colette? The one from the reception desk? Who'd carried her skis in the snow? Whom she'd just thrust money at?

She'd been expecting an older man, a businessman. Not *this* man?

*Earth, swallow me up now.*

Then it occurred to her that he must have misunderstood her. 'I mean the *owner*...' She checked her phone again. 'Yes. LeFevre. I need to speak with him.'

'Still me.' He nodded. 'Everyone calls me Matt.'

Her stomach tightened. 'You own this resort?'

'Yes. Is that a problem?'

*Inconvenient.* Especially when she'd thought he was eye candy. And kind. She couldn't do kind or attraction to someone she worked with. To anyone, really, but definitely not a colleague. 'You're so...it's unexpected. I imagined someone older.'

'I'm thirty-four.' His eyes sparkled in amusement. 'How old is old enough, in your opinion, to own a business?'

'I…um.' He was right, of course, but he was also clearly enjoying her embarrassment. 'Why didn't you say something before? Last night? Earlier?' She stared at the still-outstretched hand and shook it, but her heart wasn't in it. The coins glinted, mocking her. 'Is this some sort of game? Embarrass the new staff? A silly induction by baptism of fire? Make a fool out of me?'

'No.' His smile faded instantly. 'That was not the plan. Not at all.'

'I am not a fool, Mr LeFevre. You could at least have introduced yourself last night.'

'I tried.' He shifted in his seat. 'But you didn't give me the time of day. I offered to carry your bags, but you refused. I suggested one of my staff help you to your chalet and you snapped. I invited you to the drinks I'd arranged to welcome you, so you could meet the rest of the staff and be properly introduced to everyone. Including myself.'

She'd been exhausted, distracted by her reasons for coming here, second-guessing whether it had been a good idea. Clearly, it hadn't. 'At any point you could have said something.'

'What would that have achieved? I would have embarrassed you, which I did not want to do, but would it have changed your attitude?'

'My attitude?' Shock ricocheted through her. No. She could not be attracted to this man.

'This is my resort, Dr Tait, and I am very careful of its reputation.' He didn't match her tone, keeping his soft and low. But there was steel there, too. He was a man who liked to be in control. 'If you're going to be rude to my staff, I have to worry that you'll also be rude to my guests.'

'I treat everyone the same.'

'Then we're in big trouble. At Sainte Colette we pride ourselves on warm hospitality.' He put emphasis on *warm* as he steepled his fingers in a headteacher kind of way.

She leaned forward and matched his disapproving gaze with one of her own. 'And I treat everyone professionally. I apologise that I didn't feel like having drinks with strangers when I'd had a long journey and was exhausted. But trust me, I will treat my patients with the respect they deserve.'

Yes. Big mistake to come here. She hadn't even started the job and she was clashing already. This man certainly brought out her combative side. How had she thought he was eye candy?

So, he was a good-looking guy. So, he had a mesmerising smile when he flashed it, extremely expressive, and deep brown eyes.

What the hell had she been thinking?

But she'd signed a contract, so she was going to go through with it. Unlike other people, Rachel Tait did not renege on her promises. 'I can assure you, I have been commended many times on my efficiency and accuracy in diagnosis.'

He tapped his fingertips together. 'And your bedside manner?'

'I worked in a busy emergency department—there isn't much time for a bedside manner when you're doing CPR.' But his words rattled her. She'd never had a patient or colleague complain about her manner, but…

*Cold. Aloof.* Sure, that's what her ex had flung at her, just to make himself feel better after he'd called off their wedding. She preferred independent, self-reliant. She was practical, in control, she didn't need warm fuzzies. Apparently, being able to think unemotionally and cope level-headedly was a crime.

Her throat felt suddenly tight. She took a sip of water. 'This isn't exactly the kind of start I was hoping for.'

'Me neither.' Mr LeFevre exhaled deeply and fixed his mouth into a smile that didn't reach anywhere near his eyes. 'I truly hope we've just started off on the wrong foot. I understand you were tired after your journey and I apologise if you feel the victim of a joke.'

'Not a victim, not at all.' *Never.* She sat up straight. 'Now, would you, please, give me directions to the medical centre? I think it's about time I started work.'

He frowned. 'But you haven't eaten.'

'I'm not hungry.' She picked up her cup and willed her hands not to shake. 'Coffee will suffice.'

The sooner she got out of his way the better.

'As you know, it's a slope-side resort with ski-in, ski-out facilities. Most people tend to chairlift up and ski home, but you can come back down on the chairlift, too. The medical rooms are at the top of the main chairlift, next to our Michelin-starred restaurant, shop and hire facilities. Please, come this way.' Matt walked the new doctor to the chairlift outside the reception area. He'd been initially relieved to see she'd dressed appropriately for the conditions, but that relief had been replaced by another bout of frustration with her frostiness. What was it with this woman? She pressed all his buttons.

He usually got on with everyone. He always had. Made damn sure he did. But Rachel Tait? Prickly, brittle and downright rude.

*She'd better be a damn fine doctor.*

But he needed to make this work and he believed everyone deserved a fair chance, at least for now. Further down the track he'd review her professionalism.

He waited for her to follow him on to the chairlift, then tugged the safety bar down in front of them. He watched as she settled into her seat, seemingly completely unfazed by the process.

Her hair was held back by knitted blush-coloured earmuffs which made her look younger than he'd thought she was. He pinned her the good side of thirty, unlike him. She was dressed well for the conditions in a pink gilet with fur trim, over a long-sleeved merino jumper. She'd slipped on a pale pink ski jacket just before they'd clambered on to the lift and her trousers looked warm. She also carried a backpack and he guessed she'd brought her own preferred medical equipment with her. At least she'd got the practical things right.

He drew his gaze away from her profile—which, despite everything, he had to admit was pretty good to look at—and filled her in on the job details. 'There's a small medical practice in Sainte Colette village down the mountain we can use, but when an injury is too serious, we transfer them to hospital. Sometimes, an injury may not be life-threatening, but needs immediate attention up here. We prefer to have our guests attended to wherever and whenever they need it.'

'Excellent.' A sharp nod. 'And staff?'

'We have a nurse, a part-time physiotherapist and first-aid-trained ski patrollers. We're trialling drone surveillance, too, to give us a better overview of the harder to reach off-piste areas. Some of the staff form the mountain search-and-rescue team.'

'Good.'

'It also helps if our medics are proficient skiers, in case we need to get them to the patient before transporting them on the ski mobile.'

'I am proficient.' Her breath plumed out in the frigid air. The chairlift jerked and swung in the wind, but she showed absolutely no discomfort or unease, only the frost she'd been showing since she'd arrived. 'I discussed all this with the agency.'

'Yes, I know, but I wanted to check you'd be safe. Where did you learn?'

'France, Italy, Austria, USA. Basically, I spent every Christmas and February half-term holidays on a ski slope somewhere.'

'Wow. Okay. That's a lot of skiing.'

'Yes.' She nodded and he tried to read between the lines. Most people gushed about the beautiful scenery or the rush of the downhill or reminisced about their favourite or challenging runs, talked about the après-ski, the fun, they shared stories, compared resorts. But Rachel wasn't illustrating her memories.

He got that. Sometimes you didn't want to re-live your past, but this was only a getting-to-know-you conversation. Maybe Rachel Tait didn't get to know people. Again, could be an issue with the celebrities who came here expecting personal service. 'Perhaps you'd like to join our staff ski group? We close the lifts at four-thirty, five days a week, but on Tuesdays and Thursdays we close at four and let our off-duty staff have time to enjoy a quiet resort and empty trails.'

'I'm happy to just explore on my days off. I can do more in a day than thirty minutes.' Her eyebrows rose at his expression. She raised her hand. 'I like to keep my personal time...personal.'

'I see.' Maybe she didn't play well with others.

'But I do work well in a team, if that's what you're concerned about.' Her chin rose and she stared out at the mountain range, away from eye contact.

He supposed it was refreshing to be able to be so blunt and know exactly what you wanted and didn't want. Not trying to be a people-pleaser like he was. But her forthrightness intrigued him. She wore it like a barrier along with the *keep out* sign he'd noticed last night.

His mind slid back to that one softening glimpse she'd given him. There was more to Rachel Tait than her hard veneer. Question was, did he care enough to find it?

At this point, the jury was still out. He spent all day, every day, dealing with demanding guests and knew from other, too-personal, experience that trying to find what made other people tick could lead to pain. He didn't have the energy to go deep digging into his staff's psyches, too.

The chairlift slowed, they dismounted on to

hard, packed snow and made their way to the cluster of buildings off to the right, to be met by Alfonse, their head chef, running out of the medical room and almost careening into them. One of his hands was wrapped in a red towel and he was pale, gritting his teeth. He spoke in rapid French. 'Where the hell are the medics?'

'The medical centre doesn't open for another twenty minutes. What's wrong?'

'My hand.' He lifted it for Matt to see and he realised that the towel wasn't actually red, but was white stained with blood. A lot of blood. He beckoned Rachel closer. 'This is the new doctor. She'll take a look. Rachel...'

'What's happened?' She looked from Alfonse and back to Matt. 'We'd better get the medical centre open.'

As they rushed into the medical rooms Matt translated Alfonse's French. 'Carving knife slipped and cut across his palm. He says it's deep.'

'Okay.' She nodded, completely devoid of emotion as they settled their patient on to the gurney in the treatment room. 'Let's see what you've done.'

She took Alfonse's hand and slowly unwrapped the towel. The cut was indeed deep, showing things underneath the skin that no one should ever see. Matt swallowed and glanced at her expression. She remained impassive but said, 'Impressive work, Alfonse. It's deep and going to need some stitches. Looks like you might be off work for a few days.'

Matt was about to translate, but his chef nodded and replied in English, 'Just as we're starting the busy season.'

'That's for Mr LeFevre to worry about, not you. Your job is to heal.' She started opening drawers and cupboards, putting various things on to a silver trolley. 'Do you have keys for the meds cupboard, Mr LeFevre? I need some local anaesthetic.'

He dragged the master keys from his pocket and opened the cupboard.

'Now, while I'm drawing this up, I'd like you to put pressure on the wound.' Her eyes met his. Steady. Cool grey. *'Please.'*

He knew that was a nod to their earlier conversation and he felt a smile forming. She'd heard him and was trying to be polite. That was something at least.

'Okay, Alfonse. This is going to sting a little, then your palm will start to feel numb.' She took his hand and rested it on the trolley, inserting the needle.

There was a sudden groan and Alfonse slumped forward, sending the trolley flying sideways. Without missing a beat Rachel stopped the trolley with her hip, caught their patient in her arms and gently laid him back on the gurney. 'Mr Le-

Fevre, lower the headrest. He's fainted. We need to get him stable and safe. And put a pillow under his knees—'

Just as Matt was lifting Alfonse's leg the phone rang. She nodded for Matt to answer it, obviously used to having colleagues do the minor stuff. He was okay with that, but he sighed at the message. Another injury. Never mind that he had other work to do. 'A what? Yes, the new doctor is here. Bring them down.'

Pausing from taking Alfonse's pulse, she looked over at him. 'What is it?'

He regarded the unconscious patient and the blood now dripping into a kidney dish. 'One of the ski patrol team has rolled a snowmobile and hurt his ankle. They're bringing him in now.'

'We don't have room in here for more than one patient. There's no privacy. When he gets here, put him in the physio room. *Please.*'

He'd only brought Rachel up here for a quick tour. 'When the nurse gets here, she can do it. I've got a meeting—'

The door flew open and one of the guests, Bianca, a supermodel known only by her first name, rushed in with blood gushing from a gash under her eye. 'Stupid bloody people should watch where they're going when they're carrying skis.'

Matt's heart rate doubled. He couldn't remember a day when they'd had more than a handful of medical issues over eight hours. The medical centre hadn't officially opened, yet they already had a queue.

Where was the nurse? Thank God Rachel was here.

She blinked up at him, entirely calm. 'Grab some gauze and press it on the wound.' Then she turned to Bianca and gave the world's most famous face a nod with no hint of recognition. 'I'm afraid there'll be a bit of a wait. You'll have to sit out in the office until I'm done here. Hold the gauze on the cut until I come through, okay?'

'Why can't you do it now?' The model bristled. 'How long will I have to wait?'

'As long as it takes. I have to prioritise by severity of emergency.' No apology, but also enough authority for Bianca to take note. Rachel returned her attention to Alfonse.

'I'm doing a magazine shoot tomorrow. I can't do it with a swollen eye.' Bianca had edged towards the door, but had stopped to examine her reflection in a mirror over the washbasin. 'Will I need plastic surgery?'

Rachel raised her head from assessing Alfonse and gave the model a brief incredulous look that said, *Why are you still here?* But then her expression smoothed. 'I'll examine it thoroughly when I come through to the other room. They'll have great make-up to cover it, I'm sure. Now please, wait next door.'

Matt was impressed. Instead of snapping, as he might have done under the circumstances, Rachel's tone was firm and polite, but also authoritative.

'All the make-up in the world won't cover up this swelling.' Bianca blinked back tears as her lips formed a pout and Matt wondered if she'd ever been asked to wait for anything in her life before. Supermodel she might have been, but Alfonse needed privacy and Rachel needed space. He stepped in. 'Come with me, Bianca. Let's get that gauze on it.'

Rachel looked up from taking the blood pressure on a now semi-conscious Alfonse. 'Actually, put ice on, too, if you have some.'

'Yeah. I think we have enough ice, thanks.' He grinned and she followed his gaze outside to the snow.

'Yes. Of course.' But then she seemed to realise he was trying to make a joke and her lips curled upwards into a smile. 'Ha! Fill your boots...or rather, a plastic bag.'

For a moment he was struck dumb. Not just because she smiled and he hadn't seen her do that before, but because her whole face transformed. The ever-present two lines on her forehead smoothed away to nothing. Her eyes lit up, turning from guarded grey to a glittering silver. And her mouth...

*God.* That mouth was divine. It was like looking at a different woman. Another softer, prettier, enchanting woman. His body prickled and the strangest thought slid into his head. How would she react to a kiss…?

She was looking at him, too, her gaze snagged on his. Those beguiling eyes misted, as if she'd been struck by the same crazy idea as his, then she looked completely shocked before she erased all emotion from her face. She turned her attention back to Alfonse and the heat he'd felt dissipated.

He'd been imagining it, right? That brief connection? He snapped back to reality. The supermodel was staring at him with frank displeasure and the doctor's cheeks had turned a shade of bright red. *Not good.*

'Okay, Bianca. Let's go sort out that cut.'

Rattled by the sudden rush of desire, he ushered the world's second-most beautiful woman out of the room.

And left number one to deal with his injured chef.

# CHAPTER THREE

TEN HOURS LATER Rachel stared at the pictures on her digital tablet on the table in front of her and pressed her hand to her heart, trying to stop it beating so fast. As if that was going to work.

She blinked quickly to stop the tears from dripping on the tablecloth. *You can't cry in a restaurant, you daft thing.* She sniffed. Used the starched white napkin to dab her eyes. *Stupid. Getting emotional over him.*

Maybe it was the drain of the first day at work, getting to know where everything was kept, meeting new colleagues. Maybe it had come from the start of the day and that brutal conversation with Matthieu about her manner. The embarrassment about the tip.

Whatever it was, something was making her feel more wobbly than usual.

She stared at the photo and wondered why it made her feel so wretched when she knew she was better off without David. But she knew why; here he was with another woman on his arm, flaunting their mutual adoration for the world to see, the other woman being a colleague and friend of them both. He'd moved on. She felt betrayed.

*No emotions, remember? Where's that Ice Queen spirit you've been chasing since the break-up?*

She cleared her throat, sat up straighter. Anyway...she'd moved on, too. Here she was, in beautiful Sainte Colette. She was almost tempted to put up a photo of herself at the ski resort, but that would only be sour grapes. She knew she was okay and that was all that mattered.

'Good evening, Dr Tait.'

*Damn.*

She flicked off the social media page and turned towards the voice. Matthieu LeFevre.

*Because the first person you want to see when you feel wobbly is the boss who already thinks you're unsuitable for the job.*

'Good evening,' she replied in French. 'Call me Rachel, please.'

Had he seen what she was looking at? Irritation shivered down her spine, along with something else. For a moment, in the medical room this morning, something weird had happened. She'd looked up at him and been unable to look away. Something about the way he was looking at her, the way the golden mountain light through the window had illuminated his face, he'd looked simply beautiful. Astonishing.

She'd been captured by his gaze. It had heated

her from the top of her head right down to her toes. Hot enough to melt all that ice he'd been talking about. For a nano-second she'd slid into the feeling, then had quickly remembered she was very definitely never mixing work with pleasure again, plus they had a room full of patients. That was so not the kind of professional she was.

'Good evening, *Rachel*.' He leaned on the chair opposite her, slipping back into English, and glanced at her tablet. 'How is your evening going?'

'Perfectly fine, thank you.' She swallowed away the tight knot in her throat and nodded. One day she would encounter this man and be perfectly serene instead of mixing him up with staff or being caught in an emotional state over her ex. To deflect the conversation from herself she gestured towards her empty plate. 'The lamb was delicious.'

'I would hope so. We don't win awards by serving bad food.' Without being invited, he pulled the chair out and sat opposite her. He was so damned sure of himself it bordered on offensive. 'I wanted to catch up with you to find out how the rest of your day went.'

'It was fine. A handful of the usual twists and sprains as you'd expect here. A concussion. A couple of cuts and bruises. Three evacs from the slopes which I triaged and sent to hospital: a dislocated shoulder, an open tibula shaft fracture and

a probable ACL tear. Nothing I couldn't handle.'
Like him, she was sure of her work. Extremely.

An eyebrow rose. 'Excellent. Both Suzanne
and Eric said you found your way around easily.'

'Suzanne is an excellent nurse and Eric is a
very experienced physiotherapist. I think we'll
make a good team.'

'I hope so. The morning was a real baptism by
fire, but you handled it well.'

'That was nothing compared to Leeds Emergency Department on a Saturday night. You don't
get a chance to catch your breath. You roll from a
road traffic accident, to a stabbing, to a birth, then
a drug overdose. Everything and anything.' She
realised she was burbling on. He wouldn't care
what Leeds ER was like. She reminded herself
of his words at breakfast. 'How was my bedside
manner? Did I pass?'

If he noted the renewed frostiness in her voice,
he didn't show it. 'The way you dealt with Bianca
was exceptional. Firm but fair.'

'The same way I deal with everyone in the ER,
although I note she wasn't happy with the wait.
But you have to prioritise by need, not by who can
ask the loudest. Bianca's need was not as great as
Alfonse's even though she thought it was. Is she
famous? Only, judging by the way the team re-
acted to her later, I got the impression everyone
knew who she was.'

'You really don't know?' He leaned back in his chair and regarded her.

'No. Why?'

'She's one of the most famous women in the world. On the cover of most magazines.'

'I don't read them. I don't have time for that.' Even tonight she'd only taken a brief break from reading up on some papers about anaesthetic developments in trauma settings and opened her social media pages to see what her friends had been up to back in Leeds. 'She is very beautiful.'

'And, because of your suturing skill, she will remain so.'

And remain self-absorbed, too, because, it appeared, no one ever said no to the woman. 'Cosmetic appearance is always a high consideration with facial lacerations, but I also have to think about wound management, infection risk and any deeper tissue or bone injuries that may also have occurred. Or should I put appearance higher up the list just because someone is pretty?'

'Of course not. However, you need to know that most of our guests are on the front of magazines for one reason or another. Either beautiful or rich. Or both.'

She shook her head. 'Is that supposed to impress me?'

He visibly bristled at that suggestion. But there he was, sitting opposite her in a dark grey business suit that looked as if it had cost a fortune.

And also made him look seriously sexy…and sex-ily serious.

*Oh, dear.* Had she really just thought her boss was sexy? Twice?

*No. No. No.*

'Like you, I aim to treat everyone the same.' He regarded her steadily. 'But wealth and beauty impress a lot of people. Clearly, not you.'

'Why should it?' She clamped down on the swell of a sudden desire-fuelled panic. 'We all work hard in our chosen fields. Why does being on the cover of a magazine make someone more important?'

'Actually, it doesn't. Not at all. No more im-portant than the chefs and the housekeepers and the lifties. But celebrities are my core clientele because it's the world I walked in for a while. I know what they like, what they expect, et cetera. They also pay the bills so I can pay my staff.'

She glanced round at the luxurious touches in the room. The dark wood walls, crisp white linens and sparkling tableware. The ever-attentive wait-ing staff, the plush decor of gold-coloured velvet curtains and matching upholstery. The hushed tones, the emphasis on exemplary service.

Embodied by this man and yet, if what he was saying was true…it was just a job. Business. Yet, she could see he carried the weight of it all.

Who was he?

It wasn't her usual style to encourage conversation, but something about him made her want to know more. About his business, of course, her place of work. And not for any other reason. 'So, you're on the rich list, too?'

'Not quite.' He laughed wryly. 'Actually, not at all. But I get by and things here are going from strength to strength. Third season in and we're doing better than last year, which did better than the year before. But there's always room for growth. I'm not going to rest until the resort has reached its full potential.'

'How do you know so many rich people? I mean, some of my colleagues are doing okay, but not enough to afford a ski resort with its own lake and chairlifts, and probably not enough to even holiday here.'

'My previous business was a tour guide agency for celebrities, based in Paris. I employed people that took actors, musicians, models, to wherever they wanted to go. I made the whole thing happen: sourced the exclusive accommodations, researched the best local activities, kept everything moving so the celebrities didn't have to make any decisions they didn't want to make. When I came back here, I thought this old place had potential and I put what I knew, together with a business proposal, to an old friend. He gave me some backing which helped secure a loan. And here we are.'

'So, you gave up basically full-time holidaying to come and work here. Why?'

'Hey, it wasn't a holiday for me. I spent most of my time in the office doing all the co-ordinating, smoothing things over for my teams on the ground. Although, it did have some perks—I got to know people in the entertainment industry, got invited to parties, vacations on yachts, film festivals. All very attractive to a twenty-something from the countryside.'

'You clearly enjoyed it.' He was grinning at the memories and that did something fizzy to her gut. She wasn't sure she liked the fizz...it made her feel edgy and she liked to be in control. 'Why give it all up?'

Why did she care?

She didn't. She just wanted background information on her boss.

'I was born in the village of Sainte Colette and grew up around here, skiing and hiking in the mountains and swimming in the lake. Back then, the Sainte Colette resort barely existed—just a few basic ski huts used by the locals and a rudimentary lift. It was a good place to grow up, but, like everyone, I dreamt of escaping. I took a chance I was offered and stayed away for a few years. But then...' His eyes darkened as his words slowed. He shifted in his seat and didn't meet her eyes. 'It was the right time to come home.'

*Home.* She wondered how that felt. To have one place where you felt completely secure.

But Matt looked away and for the first time

since she'd met him she saw shutters slide up. Then he pushed his chair back and stood, giving her a quick sharp bow, abruptly saying, 'I have taken up enough of your time, Rachel. Good evening.'

So, whatever Matt's reasons were for giving up the globetrotting lifestyle, he wasn't going to share them with her. Which, of course, as a scientist who liked getting to the bottom of puzzles and challenges, made her want to know even more.

But she'd be mortified if he pushed her for personal information, so she let it go, let him go. Leaving her with a lot more questions than answers.

He was rattled.

She'd looked at him with those piercing eyes and asked him why he'd come home and he'd almost told her. Almost spilled his guts to frosty Rachel Tait. And then what?

Watch her trample all over his past? No, thanks.

Their conversation last night had started hesitantly and with difficulty, as every conversation with her seemed to, but when she forgot about being frosty, he found her questions intelligent, her conversation interesting. Until she strayed too close to his personal life.

His thoughts seemed to return to her too frequently and he couldn't understand why. Sure, she was different to every woman he'd ever dated—

not that he had a type as such. But he usually went for someone fun loving, chatty and sociable like him. Rachel wasn't bubbly and outgoing, she was reserved and independent to the point of appearing to be indifferent. She certainly wasn't a team player as far as he could see.

'Boss? You okay?' Cody, one of his team, shouted over the roar of the snowmobile engine, bringing Matt back to the present. En route to an evac on the Home Run.

He gave Cody a thumbs up. 'Great.'

Not great, when he should have been looking for the injured party instead of being intrigued and distracted by a colleague. The snowmobiles bumped up the nursery slope and underneath the chairlifts, slowly climbing their way up the mountain.

Further up, sitting on the ground, was a little girl with a pale, tear-stained face, her little chest rising and falling rapidly as she silently sobbed. Her father was sitting next to her, waving to them as they approached.

Matt jumped down from the snowmobile and recognised the man immediately. 'Michael. Hello.'

The man peered up, ashen-faced, but as soon as he saw Matt he relaxed. 'Matt. Thank God.'

'What's happened?' Matt put his hand on the man's shoulder in a gesture of solidarity, knowing too well, from personal experience, how worrying about someone you cared for ate away at you. Guilt that you couldn't help, couldn't fix them, did that, too. Then he crouched down to look at the little girl. 'Isla, sweetie. What have you done?'

'Snowboarder took her out. Damned idiot.' Michael shook his head, distress swirling in his eyes, his voice barbed and angry. 'They should be banned from the mountain.'

'Accidents happen, no matter how experienced.' Matt nodded, well aware that Michael's anxiety fuelled his words. That, and the fact he was renowned in the film world as a genius director, but outspoken and difficult to work with.

Michael smoothed his daughter's hair down. 'She says her knee hurts.'

'Okay. We just need to check her over to make sure she hasn't injured her neck or back, then we'll shoot down to the medical centre for the doc to take a look. Won't take a minute.'

'But…' Michael's jaw tightened and he looked as if he was about to complain about something, but he nodded. 'Please hurry. She's cold. We both are.'

'I know. But I'm not prepared to take any risks. I have to assess her first. We'll be as quick as we can.' Matt nodded to his colleague. 'Cody, grab some emergency blankets, please.'

Between them Matt and Cody wrapped their clients up in the foil thermal blankets and Matt spoke above the crinkle-crackle noise that was made every time one of them moved. 'Should have you both warmed up in no time.'

Michael shook his head as he looked at Isla's tear-stained face. 'My wife is going to kill me.'

So, it wasn't just his child he was concerned about. Matt sighed. 'It was an accident. She'll understand.'

'You think?' Michael raised his eyebrows, his tone turning tense. 'She's going to blame me. She always does.'

Matt glanced at the little girl who was staring up at her father and his heart went out to her. He really hoped she wasn't going to start blaming herself for whatever was going down in her parents' marriage.

'Hey, it was just an accident, sweetie.' He gave her a smile, then lifted her gently on to the snowmobile and headed back to the medical room. Wondering how his new doctor would react to a concerned father who had a reputation for outbursts and expected everyone to do his bidding.

That said, it would be a good opportunity to see her professionalism and tact in action when pushed. Because he had no doubt that Michael's good behaviour was starting to fray.

He wheeled the stretcher through to the medical room and found Rachel in the office.

She jumped up as soon as she saw him, her

cheeks flushing. 'Matt? You're doing the evacuations today?'

He nodded. 'We have a roster. Management are on it, too. We all pitch in.'

'I didn't realise.' She focused on the girl. 'Hello there. Been in the wars?'

'We've just picked this little one up on the Home Run. She got in the way of a snowboarder who took her out. She's complaining of a sore knee. No other obvious injuries.'

'Ouchy.' Rachel winced and gave the little girl an empathetic smile. 'What's your name, honey?'

'Isla,' Michael butted in and added with emphasis, 'Isla MacKenzie.'

It astounded Matt that Rachel didn't know the girl's name, although why would she if she didn't read the gossip pages? But this girl was one of the most famous kids in America, if not the world. Everyone had watched the social media posts sent live from her mother's hospital bed five years ago as she gave birth. There'd even been lucrative betting on the name choice.

'Hey, Isla.' Rachel tilted the girl's chin to look into her face. 'My name's Rachel and I'm a doctor. I just want to have a look at your leg so we can work out how to fix it. You want to come sit on here?' She patted the gurney and Matt lifted the little one over on to it. Rachel glanced up at him. 'Thanks, Matt.'

The tone was a form of dismissal, but he decided to hang around a few moments longer to ensure they could all cope with Isla's situation. Michael was fractious at the best of times and, showing no flicker of recognition, Rachel clearly didn't know she was dealing with a famous film director who was used to being surrounded by *yes* people. Rachel was definitely not a yes person. Neither was Matt—boundaries were important, after all. But if they could get through this and still have a paying guest that would be good.

She bent to talk to Isla as the door flew open and Bianca bowled in.

*Déjà vu.*

Rachel glanced over to her. 'Ah, yes. Your suture-check. Could you please wait outside? We're just dealing with an emergency.'

'But—' The model ran over to the gurney.

Rachel sighed and her tone was one of frustration. 'Bianca, please. Not again. This is a medical room, you have to wait your turn.'

'And this is my daughter.'

'Ah.' Rachel's eyes widened as she looked at mother, then daughter, and then nodded. 'Sorry. I didn't realise.'

'Where have you been? Under a rock?' Bianca threw back at her, then whirled round to Michael, who had taken a seat close to Isla's head. 'What the hell happened?'

The film director raised his eyes from the

phone he was scrolling on. 'She got taken out by some lunatic on a snowboard.'

Bianca gripped her daughter's ski jacket lapel as she scanned the little face. 'She looks okay. No damage to her beautiful face.' She pinched the little girl's cheek gently.

'It's her leg that hurts,' Michael deadpanned.

A roll of those famous large hazel eyes. 'I thought you said you could manage.'

'I can manage. It's snow, Bianca. People have accidents all the time.'

'I bet you weren't watching her properly.'

'At least I was with her. I wasn't swanning about having my picture taken.'

Matt stepped forward, about to ask them to quieten down, but was beaten to it by Rachel who glared at them. 'Quiet, please. I am trying to do an examination here. Of your injured daughter.' She turned her back to the bickering adults, almost as if shielding her patient from them, then she unbuckled Isla's ski boot Velcro. 'Let's just take this off first, honey. I'll go slowly, but tell me the moment it hurts.'

Bianca's voice rose. 'It's my *job,* Michael. It's why we're here.'

'Oh.' Michael's voice took on a sarcastic tone. 'And I thought we were here for some family time. Silly me.'

Matt watched as Rachel's shoulders tensed, but she continued to carefully slide Isla's boot from her foot while the little girl looked from her mother to her father and back again as if she were watching a tennis match. Worse, she didn't even look as if this was anything out of the ordinary. As if this happened every day.

Rachel's voice was calm and reassuring as she said, 'Good girl. My, you're brave. Can you point to where it hurts?'

'My knee.' Isla pointed.

'You okay if I take a look now? I'll try not to tickle.'

The little girl nodded, but her bottom lip began to tremble. 'It hurts.'

'I know, honey.' Rachel stroked the girl's hair. She was different today. Softer. Was it because of their conversation last night? But Matt doubted she'd change her approach because of a word from him. 'If you like, we can give you some painkillers. I'll check with your parents, first. Then, if I can have a quick look at your knee, I'll know how to fix it, okay?'

'What exactly are you going to give her?' Bianca's tone was accusatory.

Rachel blinked. 'Just some painkillers.'

'Yes.'

'No.'

Both parents answered at once.

'No.' Bianca shook her head vociferously. 'We eat clean and we don't do drugs of any kind. Ever. Do you have arnica?'

'For a ruptured tendon? That's ridic...' Rachel caught Matt's gaze and clamped her mouth shut. He just knew she'd been about to say ridiculous which would have inflamed an already volatile situation.

Instead, she smiled...and it almost looked genuine. 'I completely understand your concerns and I never suggest giving drugs to a child unless they need them. But, you can see she's in a lot of pain and it really will help.'

Silence hung thick and heavy.

Rachel looked at them one at a time. Waiting. 'The sooner we give them, the quicker they'll work.'

'Okay, but she's allergic to nuts and eggs, so you can't just give her anything.' Bianca threw her husband a sarcastic look. 'I bet you've forgotten that little fact about your daughter?'

'Of course not. I was just about to mention it. We went for lunch today and she survived, didn't she?' He snarled. 'Daddy managed.'

'Oh. You didn't wait for me so we could eat together? Gee, thanks.' Bianca folded her arms across her chest. 'So much for *family* time.'

'I can't help it if you're always working.'

'Says the guy who's always away working on a film.'

'You say that as if it's a bad thing. My films are important.' Michael's chest puffed out a little.

'They win awards. They're intelligent and con-sidered.'

'Oh, please.' The model's hands rose in exas-peration. 'Don't go on about your social justice campaigns again. Give us all a break.'

Matt couldn't and wouldn't take any more of this.

This was why he tried not to get personally in-volved with the clients. Why he'd chosen to head up the office in Paris instead of going on all those tours, because there was something about their outrageous demands that triggered something deep inside him. He wouldn't pander to their whims and definitely not to the detriment of a child.

That poor kid shouldn't have to listen to this, Rachel couldn't do her work properly.

He had to do something. 'Enough!'

'Stop!' Rachel ordered at the same time, put-ting her hand up to silence them all. Her tone gave them absolutely no question as to who was in charge here. 'I'm trying to assess this child. She's in pain and you're making it worse. Can you stop this bickering and please take her into consideration? She is the most important person in the room right now. Not any of you.'

They all stared at her, mouths open.

'If you can't speak nicely to each other, one of you will have to wait outside,' she continued, as she marched both Michael and Bianca towards the door, herding them along with her hands and then added quietly, 'I won't ask Isla to choose which parent gets to stay because that's not fair on her. So, be grown-ups and decide. Quickly.'

*Whoa.* He hadn't expected that. Matt gave her a mental fist bump while simultaneously wincing at how she was speaking to his paying guests. He admired her strength and forthrightness. And the way she was looking at the little girl, with such empathy and concern, made his heart hurt. She was like a mama bear protecting her young. Her grey eyes sparkled with fury and a gauntlet. Steel. Polished silver. Magnificent.

He looked at the two superstars who now turned to him with fire in their eyes and wondered what it would take to smooth this over for everyone. And whether he even wanted to.

'Are you going to let her speak to us like that?' Michael huffed.

Rachel had been firm, but they had been downright crass to argue like that in an emergency situation concerning their five-year-old child. Matt kept his voice low. 'I won't tolerate a challenge to my medical team. Any of my team, for that matter. This is a medical room and we need peace and quiet. One of you can stay in here, the other will have to wait outside.'

Michael frowned. 'But—'

'One of you.' With a heavy heart he envisaged his bottom line dropping because of this, but what was money compared to Isla's safety and upholding his team's respect? 'Or both of you. Feel free to leave.'

Bianca glared at her husband and shrugged. 'Okay. I'll go.'

Even that backdown seemed like point scoring. She pulled a mobile phone from her pocket and held it in front of Isla. 'Can I just…take a quick snap. Isles, baby, look up at Mommy. There. Let's see how many likes you get for a poorly leg. That'll make everything better.'

'Leave. Now.' Rachel's tone was dangerous and, even from this distance, he could see she was trembling.

The supermodel bristled. 'What? How dare—'

Rachel held her hand up again, caught Matt's eye again and added, *'Please.'*

Once Bianca had left the room Rachel's shoulders relaxed and she breathed out, put her focus firmly and completely on the child and restarted her assessment.

And Matt just stood there, lost for words. He'd thought she was cool and offhand and rude, but the way she guarded that child was *personal*. It was the closest he'd got to seeing real emotion from her.

Was this the real Rachel Tait? Fierce and raw and strong?

He wasn't sure, but it felt as though he'd got her all wrong.

# CHAPTER FOUR

SHE WANTED TO SCREAM.

She wanted to shout and stamp her feet. To put her fingers in her ears, as she had so many times when she'd been Isla's age, and pretend she couldn't hear the constant slurs, attacks and bickering. Pretend the world she lived in was happy and bright and not exploding into ugliness.

But she was a doctor now and these weren't her parents. She had to be professional and responsible and act like a grown-up, too. She'd thought she'd dealt with all that years ago, but watching that little girl's impassive face while her parents had argued around her had brought the memories rolling back, hitting Rachel square in the chest.

She hated emotions. They got in the way. They whipped the ground from under her feet and made her see things subjectively instead of objectively. And she couldn't do that. Would not allow that.

Having put Isla's leg into a temporary splint and checked Bianca's sutures, she sent them all away to get a scan on the knee. Then she breathed out and took a moment to centre herself by looking out of the window on to the ski field. The sky was a brilliant blue and there wasn't a cloud anywhere. She could hear laughter and chatter…

'Well, that was intense.'

*Matthieu.*

Her spine prickled.

She'd watched him walk the guests out, but he must have come back into the room. No doubt he was about to reprimand her for what she'd said and done. There was no way she could let him see her discombobulated.

She took one more deep calming breath, then turned to him. Ready. Her voice completely steady. 'A couple of things.'

He stepped back, frowning. 'Okay.'

'I don't like feeling as if I'm constantly being judged by you. Being careful about what I say or do in case my bedside manner doesn't make the grade.'

'I'm not judging you.' His hands rose in a gesture of submission.

'It feels as if you are. Every time I speak to a patient or staff member you look as if you're holding your breath, waiting for me to mess up. I get it. It's your business and you want it to be successful. You think I'm a loose cannon or just downright rude. But the medical room is my domain, Mr LeFevre. I get to set the tone. I've dealt with many patients in many different scenarios. I know that tensions run high and I expect that. I expect to have anxious and worried parents. It's only natural.' Natural to most parents, anyway. 'But that poor girl. Her parents were horrible. Clearly, point scoring is a game to them. Being discreet isn't. Putting their child first isn't. Taking photos to post on social media? Really? Hoping to get more likes? I'm speechless.'

'Clearly, you're not.' The corners of his mouth twitched, but he wrestled them back into a serious line. 'Isla MacKenzie is a social media phenomenon on her own. She has only ever known her parents as ultra-famous. A film director father who had a string of high-profile flings before settling down with a world-famous supermodel. Little Isla was probably the most anticipated birth after the royal family's babies.'

'I don't care. She's five years old.' Rachel took another breath. 'You know what? I realise now that I don't treat everyone the same. That girl needed extra care because her parents weren't going to give it to her. And I'm not going to apologise for what I said to them. I don't care how much money they have or who they are, she needed someone to be her advocate, because clearly neither of them are up to the job.'

'That's what made the difference, then. The child.' He said it so quietly she thought she might have misheard. Then he smiled. 'So, Dr Rachel Tait does have a heart after all.'

Her stomach did a weird flippy thing at that smile.

Which was ridiculous. Because Matthieu LeFevre could not make her stomach flip. No one could.

'A heart?' *The Ice Queen?* 'Don't count on it. But did you see her face? Nothing. No emotion except for the pain from her injury. She was completely inured to the fact her parents were fighting. She's used to it. I bet they don't show that side of themselves on social media.' Rachel picked up the cup with the remains of the coffee she'd made before Isla had come into the medical centre and realised her hand was shaking again.

She put her coffee cup down. She really did need to get on top of this. 'They didn't care about her leg. They cared about yelling at each other, at winning the blame game or scoring points. She doesn't deserve to be ignored, Matthieu. She's a little girl. Not an adult's chattel to be argued over.'

She blinked and for one awful moment she thought she was going to cry, but she cleared her throat and shrugged back on that mask of professionalism and resolve that meant she would not show her emotions. To him, or anyone else.

Why was it starting to happen now? This trickle of feelings leaking out of her?

Sure, she'd borne witness to plenty of disagreeing parents, but the fighting today was exactly the kind of thing she'd been through. Petty. Point scoring. As she'd listened to those adults arguing, something had triggered inside her. '*So much*

*for family time!'* one of them had yelled. That
had been the only thing she'd yearned for and
yet whenever she was in the same room as both
her parents she'd been forgotten altogether. Just
like Isla.

She shook her head, swallowing back all the
emotions. Shoving them deep down inside her
and closing the lid, the way she'd done ever since
she'd been younger than that little girl.

'Are you done?' Matthieu folded his arms and
gave her a look that she couldn't read. It felt as if
he was sympathising with her. Which was totally
at odds with what she'd been expecting from Mr
Business Owner.

She met his eye. Lifted her chin. 'With what?'

'With railing at me. I'm not the one who treated
her like that. I asked them to leave, remember?'

'I am not railing.' She cleared her throat. Okay,
she was railing at him. And it wasn't his fault.

'You could have been more tactful, but you're
right. We can't allow that sort of behaviour in a
medical setting.' His eyes roved her face and she
saw concern there, which felt personal. 'This has
really got to you, Rachel.'

'I'm fine.' She did not need anyone to be concerned about her.

'Here we go with that again. *I'm fine. I'm fine.*
It's okay to be affected by things. You're not a
machine.'

'No, not completely.' She threw him what she

hoped was a high-beam grin. 'But it's an aspiration.'

'I don't understand you. Are you afraid of feelings, or admitting you're feeling something?'

Panic rushed through her, tightening her gut. 'I don't need to feel. I don't want to feel. I just want to do my job.'

'You do it very well.' Shaking his head, he looked out of the window. For a couple of beats he was silent then he turned back to her, eyes shining. 'I know…come outside.'

'Why?'

'After that little debacle I need some air and I think maybe you do, too.'

'I can't just leave the medical centre.' She couldn't shake the feeling that the way he'd looked at her had been personal. As if he cared…the way a friend might care for another friend. Or something…

Since her wedding fiasco she'd withdrawn into herself and neglected her friends. Not that work had given her much time for a social life and she'd always struggled to open up to people—and she would never have talked about her disastrous walk of shame back down the aisle—but she and David had had a core group of people they'd had drinks with every now and then. Friends? She'd always hoped so, but not recently. Which was her fault, she knew.

Basically, it had been hard to face them unless

through the veil of work where she'd revelled in being busy, so she didn't have to talk to them.

And now David was sharing photos of him all loved-up with one of their friends.

'Suzanne and Eric are in the office.' Matthieu shrugged nonchalantly. 'Just give me five minutes. I think it'll do you good.'

'No—'

'Look, I'm not a doctor but I do know this place has magical healing powers. So, come on. Five minutes.' He took her ski jacket from the hook and held it out to her. It looked as if she didn't have any choice, so she shrugged on the jacket and stepped out into the icy air.

They trudged along the snow, past the restaurant and people sitting out in the sunshine laughing and chatting. Then up the hill, which was slow going in thick snow.

When they got far above the buildings, to the edge of the mountain, they stopped at a fence line and gazed down the valley to the lake and beyond, to a little cluster of red-roofed buildings that made up Sainte Colette village. Majestic pine trees bordered the mountainside and jet boats skimmed along the water, leaving little white trails behind them. Everything looked fresh and clean and bright, like a piece of art that had just been painted.

The sounds from the resort faded away, along with the tension that had sunk into her bones. She leaned her elbows on the fence and hauled cool air into her lungs.

Matthieu settled next to her. Close enough that she could breathe in the tang of masculine scent. He smelt wonderful and it made her feel even more off balance than she had in the medical centre.

Not inhaling too deeply, she looked out at the lake. 'It must have been amazing to grow up with this view to drink in every day,'

'It makes everything feel better, right?' A pause. Something flickered across his eyes, then it was gone. That darkness she'd seen last night, fleeting, then wiped clear. 'Almost.'

'What do you mean? Almost?'

He hauled back on his beautiful smile, but she could see it had taken some effort. 'Not everything can be fixed, Rachel. But it certainly helps to have something picturesque to look at.'

She looked up and regarded his profile. Tall and broad. Fit. Strong jaw, aquiline nose. Long black eyelashes framing deep brown eyes. He was a handsome man, objectively speaking. Beautiful. She wanted to look away, but couldn't bring herself to.

And, yes, weirdly, looking at him helped ease this tightness in her chest. 'What happened to you?'

'Ah, you know… Nothing.'

She didn't want to pry…hell, she'd hate it if

anyone probed her too hard about her past, but she wanted to help. It felt, with Matthieu, as if they'd started out on the wrong foot, skipped normal conversation and jumped quickly to intense. Or maybe it was just the whole Isla thing had made her a bit more sensitive today. 'Hey, I'm sure it's not nothing. It's obviously important to you.'

'It's in the past.' He shrugged. 'Families are complicated.'

'Amen to that.' She paused, waiting for him to fill the silence, knowing from professional experience that many people didn't sit in absolute quiet well.

He clasped his hands together as he leaned his elbows on the fence, not looking at her. And, as she'd hoped, he filled the gap. 'My mother lived here her whole life, she loved it. She said she needed the peace and I dare say it was better for her than a city. She…she wasn't well.'

'I'm sorry.'

'It's okay. She died a couple of years ago.'

Rachel did the maths. *It was time to come home.* 'She's the reason you came home?'

'Yes.'

She sighed, impressed that he would do such a thing and yet sad for him at the same time. 'I don't know where my mother is half the time, never mind giving up my career to look after her.'

'Really?' He turned to her and his eyes had taken on such a wealth of sadness she wanted to soothe it away. 'You don't know where your mother is? Don't you talk to her? Message? Visit?'

'Not much. Like you said, it can be complicated. We're not close,' she clarified, her voice flattening the way her mood did when she thought of her parents. 'Or my dad. They've both got other families now.'

'Even so. You should see them before it's too late. You don't know what's around the corner.'

'It's fine.' She couldn't bear to see the incomprehension in his eyes. Is that what had happened to his mother? Something out of the blue? She couldn't ask him for more details because it would look like prying. But then she realised she'd used her well-worn phrase again and suddenly felt a need to explain why she must seem so cold. Why that was important she wasn't sure, but it was important. 'Honestly, it really is fine. We were never a close-knit unit and my parents split up when I was ten years old.'

He gave her a sad smile. 'That would have been hard on you.'

'It was, but it was better than them arguing all the time.' She drew her eyes away from him, because she was scared she was giving too much away.

But he gently pressed her. 'Like Michael and Bianca?'

'Kind of. Their bickering earlier just triggered something inside me.' She looked out at the view and took deep breaths, letting the beauty ease her soul as she tried to make sense of the jumble of emotions in her chest.

Matthieu sighed. 'No one wants to relive things like that. How are they now? Your parents?'

'The divorce was very bitter and still is.' She turned back to him. 'But I've dealt with it. Honestly.'

At least, she thought she'd dealt with it, until today. Worse, she could feel him looking at her, pitying her, assessing her and she knew he could see more than she allowed anyone else to see. There was just something about him that made her feel seen.

*'Tant pis.'* He kept on looking at her, his forehead furrowed. 'I am so sorry, Rachel. I brought you outside to feel better, not worse.'

'It doesn't make me feel bad, I'm just sad you lost someone you loved.'

'Me too. It was difficult.' He shook his head and for a few moments the silence descended again. But then his expression brightened. 'So... what was the other thing?'

'What do you mean?' She noted he'd deflected the conversation back to her. Clearly, his mother had suffered in some way and he had, too. But, like her, he didn't want to talk about it.

Some things were best left unsaid. She knew all about that.

He smiled at her confusion. 'You said you had a couple of things to talk to me about.'

'Did I?' The anger from before had steamed out of her and she wanted to learn more about this man, about his mother and how a bond could be so strong between two people that they'd give up everything the way he had.

But this wasn't the time. And she wasn't sure it would be wise getting to know him better. Or for him to know more about her. 'Oh. Yes. That. I guess I need to thank you for not bawling me out in front of Michael and Bianca. Thank you for your support.'

'I wanted to speak up sooner, but I also didn't want to step in because you're right, that room is your domain. And you rule it like a queen.' His eyes crinkled at the sides. He had such nice eyes. Trusting. Warm. Kind. They lit up as he spoke. 'But I couldn't stand by and let them speak to you or Isla like that. I do have a line that I draw between professional and acceptable and it takes a lot to make me step over it, but today I did.'

'I don't think I helped, though, with my outburst.' She snorted. 'I think my line is a lot more defined than yours. Or I'm a lot closer to it.'

'Not all the guests are like Michael and Bianca.'

'Good, because I don't think I can hold my tongue for four months. I think I'd explode.'

'Isn't that what you just did?' He laughed

and made an explosive gesture with his fingers. 'Boom! Run for cover, Dr Tait is blowing up.'

'Trust me, you haven't seen anything yet.' She laughed too, feeling a little freer than she'd felt for a while, also feeling a lot closer to someone than she'd felt for a long time, too. He'd taken the trouble to ask her questions without sounding too intrusive, to listen to her, and she couldn't help telling him things she normally preferred to keep hidden.

Although, that was probably not a good thing.

*You're cold and aloof and you don't let people get close.*

For good reason.

But Matthieu's eyes twinkled. 'Is that a promise, Dr Tait?'

'You'll have to wait and see.' Wait…was that… was that *flirting*? 'Er…maybe.'

His smile grew. 'Well, I definitely can't wait.'

The laughter stalled in her chest. Had he edged closer? Was she imagining it? Or had she moved?

Either way, he was closer. She could feel his warmth, his breath whispering on her skin. His scent wound round her, like a magic spell pulling her closer to him.

Since the break-up she'd thrown herself into work and closed herself off from everyone, away from prying eyes and more pain. She didn't discuss her personal life, she didn't talk about her past and she most certainly didn't do flirting.

But clearly her body did trembling and fizzing. And there was an ache deep inside her that she didn't think would go unless...unless she did something really stupid, like touch him.

His gaze caught hers. For a moment the beautiful backdrop faded from view and Matthieu LeFevre was the only thing she was aware of. Just here, in this moment.

No past. No pain. Just a man who somehow drew her out of her self-imposed prison where she felt safe and comfortable. His deep brown eyes that she could get seriously lost in. And that mouth she suddenly wanted to kiss.

*What the hell?*

That mouth shaped up into a heart-melting smile.

She swallowed back the panic rising in her throat and turned to go, but her hand brushed against his.

'Wait... Rachel...' The way he said her name... *Ray Shell*...so soft and exotic and sexy, had her keening towards him.

His fingers curled into hers and the panic mingled with the fizz that started in her stomach and spread through her, making her limbs tremble and her heart race. The sensation of his skin on hers sent ripples of heat through her. But the ache didn't go. If anything, it got worse. Until the only thing she could think about was gripping those fingers and holding on. Holding him.

*Is this the line, too? Professional and personal?*

She could not cross it. She could not get close to him. Not to anyone. She slipped her hand from his. 'I have to get back.'

And put some distance between herself and this man who made her feel things she didn't want to feel.

# CHAPTER FIVE

HE'D HELD HER hand like a smitten teenager. Grabbed on to it like a lifeline, propelled by some kind of force he'd had no control over.

He didn't get it. What was it about Rachel Tait that made him want to break down her barriers and get closer to her? She was like a complex challenge he needed to work out.

He'd managed to keep out of her way for the last few days, burying himself in his work to avoid her, but he just couldn't get her out of his head.

He sat at the bar, nursing his beer, trying to concentrate on a conversation about Christmas festivities.

'The big Christmas tree for reception is arriving next week,' Louis informed him.

'It's already a week late. We should never have paid in advance.'

'I know, they've been promising delivery for days. We'll use a different supplier next year.' Louis gave an apologetic shrug, then ran his finger down the meeting agenda in his open planner. 'And we're decided about Christmas Day, then?

A later breakfast window so families can spend family time together in their chalets, then Father Christmas after lunch once they've all come back from the mountain. I've hired the suit, so we just need to make sure it fits you.'

This was a part of the holidays Matt always loved—probably more than the kids, if he was honest. Just seeing their faces when he entered the lobby was pure magic. He knew, well enough, the ache of a difficult Christmas and if he could help make a child's day happier then he'd done his job.

He patted his belly. 'Better get some padding for it then. Where's that orange and cardamom cake you usually put out for après-ski?'

'In the fridge, help yourself. But, mate, if I had a decent pack like yours, I wouldn't be eating cake. The women love it just as it is.' Louis looked down at his own stomach, as flat as Matt's, and sighed. 'Man, I need to get some exercise.'

'You ski most days, lug crates of bottles around, carry wood. You're doing okay.' In fact, Louis was impressively fit.

'That's not the kind of exercise I mean.' His friend's eyes widened. 'Hey, we should have a night out. Get away from here where we're all about work. I can't remember when either of us last had a day off. We deserve to have some fun, maybe meet some women.' He swayed his hips suggestively. 'Have some more fun…'

Matt laughed at his friend's hopeful expression.

'Aren't we supposed to be talking about Christmas plans?'

'Yes. But I've briefly diverged on to weekend plans. Come on, Mattie. You haven't been out much since your mum died. Two years. It's time.'

And yet he didn't feel as though he'd been losing out. Which was weird, because he'd loved his old life. He'd spent most of his twenties partying, travelling the world, having a good time—a wild time even, hooking up, but he didn't much feel like playing those games any more. 'We've got too much to do here. Maybe, in the new year, we could take a trip over to Geneva or down to Nice?'

'Okay…but don't blame me if the women think you're old and boring.' Louis winked.

'At thirty-four? I prefer mature and wise. And, after this season, hopefully rich, too,' Matt shot back with a laugh. 'Believe me, I'm fine.'

He realised he was using the same words as Rachel. He meant them—did she? Was she truly fine being on her own? Dealing with everything with no support? Maybe she had support he didn't know about.

Maybe she was married or engaged or otherwise committed.

He'd held her hand.

And he was allowing her back into his head again. Why was he attracted to the woman with the biggest 'no entry' sign on her forehead?

He gave his friend a wry smile. 'Can we focus

back on the meeting and not my shortfalls as your wingman?'

'Of which there are many…' Louis grinned. 'One, you always get the most beautiful ones—'

Matt coughed. 'The meeting…?'

'Okay. We'll do your shortfalls later. But open a bottle, we may be there some time,' Louis warned through his evil grin. 'After you've done your *Ho-ho-ho* routine—probably meaning some poor kids will be in therapy for years—we'll put on the staff ski show. Then in the evening we'll just serve a buffet.' Louis checked things off against his list. 'I think that's all for Christmas Day. The plans are all set up for New Year's Eve. The band have confirmed and the ticket sales are going well.'

'Excellent. Right, back to work.'

'Yes, boss.' Louis gave him a swift jokey salute. 'Oh, and we need to reschedule the welcome drinks for the new doctor. She's been here a week and we still haven't organised anything.'

And just like that, she was at the front of his mind again. Along with the sharp tang of desire that seemed to kick into action whenever she was near. 'I don't think she's keen.'

'Not keen for a party? Who is this woman?'

Rachel Tait. An enigma. 'It's her call. Not everyone's a party animal like you, Louis—'

Fast footsteps thumping down the tiled corridor had them both turning towards the door.

'Hey, boss! Can you help?' It was Frederik, breathless and red-faced. 'We've got a collapse in reception.'

'Did you call Rachel? The doctor?' Matt asked Fred as they ran towards the lobby. 'Get her down here to help.'

'We tried her cell, but she's not answering.'

'She must be somewhere. Try the restaurant.'

'Tried that. I was coming from there when I saw you in the bar.' Poor Fred was trying to keep up and failing. 'Sorry, boss.'

'I saw her heading out with skis a few hours ago,' Louis said. 'Around lunchtime.'

Matt glanced out the huge picture window that ran along the corridor and out to the dark night. 'And she's not back yet?'

'Search me.' Louis shrugged. 'What about Suzanne and Eric?'

'They went home, back down the mountain.'

'Looks like it's just us, then,' Louis said. 'The A Team.'

'Totally, we'll deal with it.' As head of the first-aid responder team, Matt was prepared for pretty much any emergency they had, but he'd have preferred some proper medical back-up, too.

They turned the corner to see a body on the floor in the recovery position and a woman Matt knew was Rita Marsh, a TV soap opera actress, kneeling next to him. As he got closer he could see her body was rigid with panic while her son's seventeen-year-old body jerked and twitched.

Thankfully, Zoe was keeping onlookers at bay. There was nothing worse than having gawkers in situations like this.

Rita looked up as they approached, the agony of worry etched across her face. 'Please help us. Zane's diabetic. His sugars are very low.' She showed them a small hand-held monitor. Sure enough, the readout showed life-threatening blood sugar scores.

'Get a privacy screen,' Matt called to Zoe, then knelt down next to the boy, checked his safety, made sure his airway was clear and that he was securely on his side. He turned to the mum. 'Do you have any glucagon?'

She looked blankly at him. 'What?'

'The sugar injections. Perhaps you were given some from the hospital or your doctor?'

'Oh, yes. Sorry, yes, we do. And insulin, too. It's all so new to us, you see. He was only diagnosed a few weeks ago and we've been in shock really. He was so sick and I thought he was getting better...' She rummaged in her ski jacket pocket and pulled out a bag of jelly sweets. 'We've got some sweets. I don't know... I don't know what to do. I can't remember what they told us.'

Matt's heart went out to her, she was clearly terrified and racked with guilt and anxiety. He made sure his voice was gentle. 'I can't give them to him while he's like this, he could choke if he can't swallow properly.'

'Oh. Yes.' She nodded. 'But the injection pen thing is back at the chalet. In his toiletries bag.'

It would have been much better if Zane had it with him, but that was a conversation they'd need to have later. Matt looked at Louis, who was talking in reassuring whispers to Zane. They always made a good tag team in situations like this and Matt thanked his lucky stars that Louis had done the same first-aid courses he had. 'Louis, go to chalet four. Grab Zane's wash bag and bring it back. Run.'

Then to Fred. 'Call the helicopter, explain the situation. Severe hypoglycaemia in a seventeen-year-old.'

Zoe slid over a screen on wheels, as fat tears slid down Rita's face. 'We should carry it with us, I know. But I thought he had it, he thought I had it. I wanted him to take responsibility for looking after his meds.' A choked sob. 'But he's still a child really and he's dealing with all the new things he needs to know about the condition.'

'It's a lot to understand and a new diabetic has to learn to be guided by how they're feeling as well as by the blood glucose readings. Add in extra exercise and that can cause a drop in sugar levels, too. He probably isn't at that point of understanding and recognising the changes yet. That's why you have to do frequent blood sugar readings.' Matt put his palm on her arm to comfort her while he watched the boy's face. He was pale and his breathing was raspy.

They needed to get the glucagon in, and quick, because if they didn't Zane could slip into a coma. Then he'd definitely need more help than Matt was able or trained to give. *Where was Rachel?*

Why wasn't she back yet? Was she okay? Was she lost? It was dark outside and no one had seen her since lunchtime. His gut tightened with a gnawing stab of worry. Something he hadn't felt in a couple of years, but was all too familiar.

He pushed it away and asked Rita, 'How long has Zane been like this?'

'Five minutes? I don't know. He said he wasn't feeling great as we came off the mountain, then he started mumbling odd things that didn't make sense. I asked if he felt it was his blood sugar, but he just snapped at me. Then he collapsed.' She stroked her son's hair. 'This is all my fault. I should have watched him better.'

'It's no one's fault. Honestly. It's a tricky thing to negotiate, particularly at the beginning.'

Fred ran back over. 'Heli's on its way with the paramedics. ETA ten minutes.'

He was swiftly followed by Louis who rushed in carrying a large leather wash bag. 'Here we go.'

'Thanks.' Matt grabbed the bag and found the orange emergency glucagon set. Clicking it open, he primed the syringe, reconstituted the little vial of powder, then jabbed the needle into the boy's deltoid muscle on his arm. 'It should only take a few minutes to work.'

'Thank God. Thank God.' Rita grasped Matt's hand as more tears spilled down her cheeks.

'But he's not going to feel great when he comes round.' Matt tried to be gentle while preparing her at the same time. 'He might vomit and he'll be groggy, but even so, he's going to need more sugar intake in the first instance. I'll get some juice organised.'

They watched and waited. Matt hoped they hadn't been too late, knowing that Zane's life could still be in danger. With all situations like this he felt as if he was holding his breath, wondering if there was anything more he should be doing, knowing he didn't have the resources or skills for much more—unless he needed the defibrillator unit.

He hoped like hell it wouldn't come to that.

Slowly, the twitching stopped and then Zane lay still, his breathing coming back to normal as the paramedics ran into the lobby. Rita's tears hadn't stopped and now they started to flow uncontrollably.

'Thank you, Mr LeFevre.' She wrapped Matt in a warm, shaky hug. 'Thank you so much.'

*See, Rachel? They aren't all like Michael and Bianca.*

He wanted her to be here to see the gratitude

and warmth. He wanted her to be here. That sent a warning alarm shuddering through his body. Maybe a night out with Louis was what he needed after all.

Once he'd handed the boy over into the paramedics' care, Matt was finally able to breathe out. Within minutes patient and parent were safely ensconced in the helicopter on the way to hospital and he retreated to the bar for a steadying drink and a debrief with Louis.

They'd managed to save the boy's life without her. But where the hell was Rachel?

Gulping down the last of his beer, he jumped off the bar stool and went to the restaurant to see if she'd somehow bypassed them, but she wasn't there. He went to her chalet, but it was in darkness and no one answered his knocking. She still wasn't answering her phone. Maybe she'd gone down to the village on the shuttle bus? But the bus driver didn't recall dropping her off.

He tried her phone again. Still no answer.

Now he was starting to get concerned. What if she'd hurt herself?

What if she'd got lost?

# CHAPTER SIX

IT WAS DARK now and the trail was lit only by the stars, a full moon and the soft glow from Rachel's head torch. But the snow reflected all available light and she could easily make out the twists and turns ahead and any bumps or crevasses to avoid.

It had been a couple of years since she'd skied and she'd felt rusty at first, but now she was totally into the groove with the wind in her hair and the cold air blasting her cheeks. Flying faster and faster down the mountain, she felt wonderfully, masterfully, fabulously free.

A loud beat blared in her headphones. *God,* she loved eighties rock music. All that angst and emotion, the awesome anthems. She joined in, singing at the top of her voice, as she whooshed through the snow and really did feel as if she was free falling through the night.

At a crossroads of two tracks she paused to get her bearings. Far below, to the left, the resort lights twinkled and winked. It looked like a pretty Christmas card and she knew the calm and comfort it held for everyone, staff and visitors alike. She felt a sudden warmth in her chest.

Home? No. She had her little flat in Leeds waiting for her...to sell, probably, given she didn't want to go back to work in that city while David was there.

So, Sainte Colette was her place, for now.

To the right, and much further away, the village lights glittered. A huge dark expanse—the lake, she imagined, loomed in between.

Which brought her right back to Matthieu and those moments by the fence the other day. His skin touching hers. The ripple of want that had slid through her. The want she'd been trying to get rid of ever since and that had prompted today's adventure to get Matthieu out of her head.

Hence the skiing. Purging her thoughts with loud music. Pushing her body to the limits with black runs that challenged her experience and took all her focus and concentration to get down.

One stop. One little stop, one moment's lapse and he'd come tumbling back into her thoughts again. She could only thank her lucky stars she hadn't bumped into him in the last few days because she just knew she'd die of embarrassment. Well...actually, she'd made sure she hadn't crossed paths with him, avoiding him any time she'd got a glimpse of that body, easy to do as he was head and shoulders above anyone else and instantly recognisable in a group.

Fancy grasping his hand like that.

Fancy wanting to kiss him.

What had she been thinking?

Nothing. That was the problem. She'd been led by her body's instinctive tug towards him. So acute she'd not been able to stop herself.

So, she'd stayed away from anywhere he might be. Turned her thoughts to anything but him.

Trouble was, no amount of avoiding him would stop the chatter in her head. Where exactly was that line he talked about? Was it talking? Flirting? Touching? More?

Did she want to cross it? Did he?

*Aargh!* Why did relationships—*people*—have to be so damned complicated? Give her science and predictable outcomes any day.

Turning the music up extra loud so she couldn't hear any more of her thoughts, she set off down the hill, setting her sights on the resort, a hot spa bath with a soothing glass of red wine and an early night.

No stopping at the restaurant on her way through, she'd make do with cheese and biscuits in her chalet.

No popping into reception. No buying a drink at the bar.

No hankering for a chat with Mr LeFevre.

A Matthieu-free zone.

That's what she needed.


He heard her before he saw her. The trudge of ski boots through the darkness. A hum…was it a hum or a wail? No, she was humming a song he thought he might recognise, but wasn't sure. She was woefully out of tune.

His brisk heart slowed. The alarm abated. She was okay.

She walked round the corner, her head bobbing to a tune he could almost hear through her headphones it was so loud. Her gaze was down, so she didn't see him. But he could see she was smiling.

The automatic light on the lintel jumped into action and she was lit by a warm golden glow. Once again, he was spellbound by her beauty. She was, unusually for her, utterly calm, her cheeks pink from exercise. Her eyes glittered— he knew exactly how that ski high felt, but his breath whooshed out of him as concern and relief took over in equal measure. 'Rachel. Hey.'

'Whoa! Matthieu?' She lumbered towards him, her gait rocky in her ski boots. Her expression had gone from pure joy to alert, personal to professional as if a switch had been flipped. 'You nearly gave me a heart attack. What's wrong? What's happened?'

She was clearly okay—more than okay, in fact. Looked as though his concern was an overreaction and now he was standing here like an idiot. He stuck to work issues. 'I thought you should know one of the guests had a seizure in reception.'

She breathed out plumes of air. 'Oh, dear. Are they okay?'

'I think so. He's gone in the helicopter to the hospital at Bourg St Maurice.'

'Okay.' She rested her skis in the rack outside her front door. 'You'd better come in.'

She swiped her key card into the lock, then lumbered into her chalet, stopping in the hallway to undo the Velcro on each ski boot and slipping her feet out. Then she hung her jacket up on the hook by the door and he followed suit with his.

The chalet was neat and tidy with no personal items anywhere, just a closed laptop on the small dining table. But the whole place smelt of her—a flowery, light perfume at odds with her strong and vivid personality. It made him feel almost light-headed to be enveloped in her scent.

She walked him through to the kitchen and flicked the kettle on. 'Right. Talk me through it.'

She clearly thought his alarm had just been about the patient and not about her. Which was a lucky escape for him. The last thing he needed was someone else to worry about.

But he knew it was guilt that fed his concern, because what if something had really happened to her and he hadn't been able to help her, or find her in time? The way he'd spectacularly failed before.

The thought that he was starting to care for Rachel spooked him. He hardly knew her, but he was strangely drawn to her. Which had to stop. He needed to dial back his reactions. Flick the same switch she had, from personal to professional.

*Work. Think about work.*

'Zane's a newly diagnosed diabetic and his blood sugar reading was very low. His mother was with him and had a glucagon injection that we gave him. We protected his airway and called the helicopter to take them to hospital.'

'Okay. Good.' Rachel took off her knitted headband and shook her hair loose. It skimmed her jawline, framing her face perfectly. 'You know a lot about it.'

'I'm a trained first aider, I need to know about these things.' And after looking after his mother most of his life he was invested in first aid. Not that he needed to tell Rachel that.

She nodded. 'You did the right thing. Completely. Sorry I wasn't around to help.'

'We called you a million times.'

'Did you? I didn't hear my phone.' She looked behind her at the looming shadow dotted with the little golden lights of the piste-grooming machines, her eyes dreamy. 'I was on the slopes.'

'On your own?'

Her forehead creased and her eyes narrowed. 'Yes?'

'In the dark?' It shouldn't matter who she skied with or when. She was a competent skier who knew the risks. Only, he owned the resort and if anything happened to her it was his business.

But it wasn't his business he was thinking about right now. It was her.

He imagined her lying on the snow damaged from a fall.

He imagined her lying in his bed.

This was crazy. And totally inappropriate.

Now he couldn't *not* think about her in his bed. Hot desire prickled through him and he almost wished he had kissed her back there on the mountain, then at least he could have expunged some of this need. Although he doubted he'd erase that need completely.

Her eyes were still dreamy as she spoke, her head clearly somewhere on the mountain. 'I had my head torch, so I was fine. It was fun up there for the sunset.' Her face lit up. 'The colours were amazing. Beautiful.'

He imagined seeing Sainte Colette through new eyes and agreed it would be magical. But to him, although it was his home, it had undertones of pain, too. And guilt. Along with immense gratitude for all the good times he'd experienced, despite the bad. So, yes, home.

She put a teabag into a mug, then looked up at him, her eyes asking a question. *You want a drink?*

And spend more time here, with her? Tempting. But that would only deepen his attraction to her.

He shook his head. He was just going to give

her some advice that he hoped he could dress up as a suggestion, then go. 'Look, there are some challenging trails up there. You might want to join the staff ski group tomorrow.'

'Oh, I don't know.' A shrug.

'They're a friendly bunch, it's a good way to meet the other staff.' He remembered she'd said she preferred to ski on her own and waited for her refusal, but she just smiled.

'Friends?' She thought for a moment, then nodded. 'Maybe.'

It was probably as good as he was going to get from her. 'Okay. Well, I should get going. Just wanted to give you a heads up about Zane for when he gets back from the hospital. In case either he or his mum needs to chat to someone who knows what they're talking about.'

'Great. Thanks. If you see him, tell him to pop by any time.'

'I will.' He turned to go, but she said,

'Matthieu…'

He whirled round. 'Yes?'

'About the other day…' There was a glimpse of softness there. Wanting.

He couldn't deny there'd been a connection up on the mountain. But did Rachel want more? What was she going to say? That she wanted to take things further? Did he?

In the past he'd only ever kept things light with women. Having his mother fill his spare time with her needs gave him precious little emotional space for anyone else. Now he was free to do whatever he wanted, but the thought of deep and meaningful gave him hives. Find happiness? When his mother never had? When the thought of him being too late to save her still haunted him?

He scuffed his hand across his hair. 'It was an intense conversation.'

'It was. Yes. That's what it was.' She exhaled, as if she'd been holding her breath waiting for his answer.

'And people do things, reach out. At times like that.' He was trying to convince himself, as much as her, that it hadn't meant anything more than a friendly hand squeeze. 'It won't happen again.'

'No. It won't.' She nodded sharply, then walked through to the front door and opened it, expecting him to leave. She was clearly used to people doing her bidding. He swallowed as something akin to disappointment ran through him. He hadn't realised just how much he'd been hoping for her to want more. Which clearly meant he did. And now he was being rejected. Okay. He could deal with that.

Looked as though he didn't have a choice.

And it was weird, because he usually only hooked up with women who thought the same way he did. But something about Rachel made him crave more of her company.

As he tugged his jacket on, she said, 'You did well today with the diabetic patient.'

'I know.' Stupid thing was, even after her rejection, he still wanted to kiss her. 'Goodnight, Rachel.'

'Goodnight.'

He stepped out into the icy night, looking back one last time.

She raised her hand in a small wave. 'Matthieu?'

Her voice was soft. Her pupils were dilated and he saw raw need there, too. It fuelled his arousal. He couldn't look away. In spite of everything he still wanted to kiss that pouting, sensual mouth. What would she taste like? Hot and spicy, he thought, just like her personality.

His heart jittered. 'Yes?'

He wondered whether she'd invite him back in, whether he'd agree. But she gave him a wavering smile. Something was making her back off and he was pretty sure it wasn't him.

'Thanks for checking on me,' she said gently, and he knew she'd worked out—or guessed—the real reason he'd been waiting for her: to make sure she was safe. 'But I can look after myself.'

Then she closed the door, leaving him hot and cold and very confused.

# CHAPTER SEVEN

EVEN THOUGH SHE liked being on her own, Rachel had to admit there was safety in numbers. Especially when Matthieu was close by.

The feelings he stoked in her were too intense for her to be alone with him again—she just knew she wouldn't be able to hide them next time. But she'd heeded his message and come along to the staff ski session.

She also had to admit that skiing in a group was fun, too, despite her earlier reservations. Five of them had met at the chairlift: Sonia from the restaurant, Louis the bar manager, Zoe from reception, herself and…of course, Mr Resort himself. She'd thought perhaps he'd come to assess her skiing skills, but, apparently, he came on these jaunts most Tuesday and Thursday afternoons just to hang out with his friends, who also just happened to be staff, too. It turned out that he employed half the village and they all thought he was a local hero for turning a struggling economy into a booming one and for bringing famous celebrities to their part of the world.

A hero? She had to admit there was a lot of good in him.

They'd taken her out on to the back trails where few tourists went and kept together as a close group. It had been wonderful to ski through unmarked snow, weaving through pine forests and look across deep valleys into neighbouring ski fields and resorts, but now they were racing down some tricky black runs on their way home and she had to concentrate hard.

Rachel followed them, happy to be the last, knowing she didn't have their skills, but glad she could keep up. Almost.

'Not bad!' Louis shouted as she reached them, breathless, looking down the hill to the resort buildings far below. A small round of applause came from the group with cheers of, *'You did well!' 'You made it!' 'Go girl!'*

'Thanks.' She caught her breath and did a jokey bow. 'I'm a bit slow, but getting there.'

She caught Matthieu's eye and he gave her a look that told her he was impressed by her skiing prowess and he was glad she'd come along. There was something exciting about his brief smile that made her feel as if they shared a secret. It slid into her chest, making her feel warm and seen. She hadn't realised before how little she'd felt seen by anyone recently. Or maybe it had been that she'd chosen not to be…she wasn't sure.

Zoe raised her ski pole and pointed off to the

side where the snow had been packed into little humps and bumps. 'Mogul run?'

'Why not?' Rachel grinned. It looked far harder than what she was used to, but she'd come to realise that these guys would talk her down, pointing out the easiest way through while coaxing her to try some of the more technical bits.

And that was exactly what they did, with whoops of encouragement. If she'd been on her own, she'd have avoided all of it, but with this group she was learning, growing. And they were all light-hearted and fun, too.

She made it safely down the moguls and they only had a couple more runs left before they reached the resort. She swished up to the back of the group and gulped in air, to find they were deep in discussion about some sort of show they were going to do for the guests.

'On Christmas Day,' Sonia explained, 'the boss dresses up as Father Christmas and we dress as his helpers and elves, reindeer, fairies, that sort of thing. And we do a skiing display down the Home Run. The kids love it.'

'The adults do, too,' Louis added with a cheeky smile. 'The ladies in particular. We're very…popular.'

Rachel ignored Louis's comment, even though she imagined anyone would love to watch Matthieu's skills.

She looked at 'the boss' and grinned. 'Father Christmas?'

He shrugged but smiled. 'What can I say?'

'I don't know?' She laughed. 'Ho-ho-ho?'

'Good one.' He guffawed, then pushed off on his right leg, then his left, and before she could say Rudolph he was skiing flat-out towards a rail. He jumped up on to it, gliding along on one ski, then he did a star jump off and something she'd only ever seen a gymnast do before that involved a sideways twist in the air, before disappearing over the edge.

With whoops and cheers the others followed one by one, doing somersaults, star jumps and twists.

'You can do this,' Rachel told herself and pushed off on her left ski, but when she got to the rail, she lost her nerve. *Hot damn.* She couldn't go back up the hill without a lot of bother so that was it. Her one chance at doing something daring.

Disappointed with herself she inched alongside the rail to the edge of the jump and saw them, below, waving at her. It was a long way down.

Thank God she hadn't actually caught the rail because she had no idea how she would have landed without making a fool of herself in front of them. In front of Matthieu.

She'd been a fool too many times before. The altar sprang to mind.

She raised her poles and waved back, but shook her head. 'I'm good, but I'm not that good! See you at the bottom!'

By the time she got down to the next run the others had all skied off, but Matthieu was waiting for her.

Her heart gave a little jolt as she skied up to him and she hoped he'd interpret her heating cheeks for exhilaration and the icy blast. He hadn't admitted that he'd been concerned about not being able to get hold of her yesterday, but he hadn't denied it either. Just the thought of someone caring enough to worry about her gave her an extra layer of warmth.

Warmth that her body interpreted as something hotter, judging by the tingles in her traitorous body. She couldn't deny she was attracted to him, but she was not going to act on it. They'd agreed. 'You should have gone with the rest, I'm fine to get down by myself,' she said.

'No one's left behind, Rachel. That's a rule of ours.' He grinned. 'Thought you might have given the rail a go?'

'Hey, I know my limits. But that was brilliant. You're all awesome.'

'You're not bad yourself.' He nodded. 'I'm happier now I've actually seen you ski. You can join the search-and-rescue team if you want.'

High praise indeed. Her belly filled with heat. 'I'd love to.'

'Excellent. I'll put you on the roster. You coming for a drink?' His eyes roved her face, and he must have seen the hesitation in her eyes because he quickly added, 'We usually stop in for one after these sessions. You're welcome to join us.'

'No, thanks.' She searched her mind for an excuse, because just thinking about the altar had made her jittery about giving too much of herself away. 'I really need to send some emails.'

He regarded her for a moment, then nodded. 'Okay. Another time, maybe?'

He didn't press her or try to convince her but then, why would he after what she'd said to him yesterday? She shut people out the moment they got close. But it was for the best. Short-term pain for long-term gain.

She had no desire to be hurt again.

A few days and another group ski session later Rachel was sitting in her usual place in the restaurant. It had been a good day. The patients hadn't been too taxing, but challenging enough. She'd even had a quick drink with the ski group which had been fun, but they'd all dispersed and she was grateful for some alone time.

Mainly because of the picture she was looking at right now.

David and Vicky at the annual hospital ball,

an event she and her ex had attended together for the last two years. She swallowed back a lump in her raw throat and, despite herself, enlarged the photo so she could see them more easily. Dressed in glamorous evening clothes, they looked absolutely besotted with each other in front of the huge Christmas tree in the hotel foyer. A place she and David had stood for photos. She still had them, on her tablet. Somewhere.

All those photos of their trips away, their little engagement party. David had been the one person she'd ever felt close to. The only person she'd allowed herself to open to…and apparently even that hadn't been enough. She'd tried…tried so hard, but some things you kept private, right? You didn't need to tell everybody everything. Maybe she should have?

And… *Oh!* Her heart squeezed as she enlarged the photo even more and, yes, on Vicky's left ring finger was a huge sparkling diamond. They'd got engaged? So soon? How so? How could two people fall for each other so quickly? Unless…

*'There's no one else. It's not that,'* he'd said, but *It's not me, it's you* was what he'd meant. Or had Vicky been waiting in the wings? Their friend… her friend really. At least Rachel had thought they were friends.

She didn't even want to think about that. One betrayal was bad enough. And she couldn't remember a time when David had ever looked at her like that, with such adoration—

'Nice-looking couple.'

'Oh!' Her heart jerked in surprise at the voice.

Matthieu, of course. She'd been so absorbed in the photo she hadn't heard him approach. She turned the tablet over so he couldn't peer too closely—not that he could miss it; she'd enlarged it to about ten times its normal size.

She cleared her throat. 'Were you looking for me? Is something wrong?'

'Not at all. I do a round of the bar and restaurant every night before I finish work, just to make sure everything is running smoothly.' He glanced back at the tablet. 'Friends of yours?'

'My ex, actually.' The words tumbled out before she could stop them. 'And his new girlfriend. *Fiancée.* Well, it looks like they're engaged. Which is quite sudden given we only broke up a few months ago.'

*Hot damn.* Why had she just told him that? But she'd been so taken aback by him being there and so derailed by the picture she'd blurted it all out.

He was going to think she was a complete flake.

'Ouch.' He grimaced and put his hand on his heart. 'That must sting.'

Sting, yes. That's how she felt. An acute stab of pain. She thought about saying *I'm fine*, but had come to know that Matthieu wouldn't accept that from her. *What to say?*

He kept on looking at her, expecting more from her. *Oh, what the hell.* She'd already been caught looking at the photos, she should probably elaborate a little more as to why an engagement could be hurtful. 'We were supposed to be getting married last July.'

'Ah.' He looked at her sympathetically. 'It's never easy.'

'On the contrary. It's getting easier by the day.'

'And yet you're still looking at the photographs.'

'I know. Stupid. But I just came across them on a mutual friend's post.' The stabbing pain was easing a little and she realised she hadn't even thought about David for a few days, until now. She didn't want him to intrude on this special place. He was her past, she needed to move on. She sat up straighter and gave Matthieu a smile she hoped was reassuringly bright. 'It was just a surprise to see them together, that's all.'

'Of course. I imagine you gave him hell?'

'For falling in love with someone else? No! What he does is none of my business.' Despite the heartache.

Two years gone, just like that. All that feeling of being part of something bigger than herself, all the belonging she'd yearned for, had thought she'd achieved, had come to nothing but hurt.

Being single could be lonely at times, but if it meant she didn't have to go through that again, then she would remain steadfastly on her own. She pushed her hair back from her face and smiled. 'Ah, well. You live and learn, right?'

'You sure do.' Matthieu gave her such an understanding smile in return she wondered if he'd ever had his heart broken. She doubted that. From what she'd heard from Louis about their past escapades, she doubted either Matthieu or the bar manager had ever loved and lost. They were all about the fun.

But he tilted his head to one side. 'Rachel, can you do me a favour?'

'Of course.'

'I've got an errand to run in the village and I need someone to give me a hand.' He lifted a large cloth sack that bulged at odd angles. 'Louis is busy, Zoe can't leave reception, it's Fred's day off. Angela—'

She shoved the tablet into her bag and stood up. 'What is it? Father Christmas duties already?'

He laughed. 'Kind of. But you'll need a warm jacket, gloves and scarf. Meet me at reception in about five minutes?'

Intrigue wound through her.

Intrigue and something altogether unexpected… excitement.

# CHAPTER EIGHT

SHE WAS BACK there in four minutes.

She followed him across the car park and over the road to a building she'd seen, but not investigated yet. Round the back she discovered a low wooden sled complete with cushions and a rug.

Frantic barking came from behind a large wooden door which Matthieu creaked open to reveal a huge barn and six beautiful husky dogs. He was immediately bombarded by them all vying for his attention, jumping and barking in excitement. He laughed at their antics and gave each of them a good rub and stroke. 'The dogs need a run and I have to send some packages from *la poste* for my guests, so I thought we could do both at the same time.'

She looked at her watch and realised it was close to seven-thirty. 'Won't the post office be closed this late?'

'Natalie's an old friend of mine. She won't mind if we call by. Come in.' He beckoned to her. 'They won't hurt you.'

'Are you sure?' But she couldn't help laughing

as one of the pups, with the most adorable golden eyes, jumped up and gently nuzzled her hip.

'I think you've got an admirer, Rachel. That's Loki.'

'As in Thor's Loki?'

'Yes. That's Thor there. And Freya, Sif, Fulla...' He made a strange half-whistling, half-clicking noise and they all gathered round him...except one. Matthieu laughed and click-whistled again. 'This is Odin. He's younger than the rest and still in training.'

'Cool names.'

'Louis is a bit of a mythology geek. We're doing Norse at the moment, but I think we're going Greek soon. He said he wants an Apollo next.'

'Perfect.' She laughed. 'They're all Louis's dogs?'

'They're our dogs.' At her frown he explained, 'We've been friends a long time. We grew up together, worked in the agency together and then he came back here a couple of years after me.'

Her heart warmed as they raced around her legs. 'They're absolutely gorgeous. Do they mind about pulling the sled? Is it hard for them?'

'Not at all. They're bred to work and to run.' He crouched down and nuzzled Odin's snout. 'They're strong and smart and they love it. That one's Freya. She's Odin's mum.'

'Hey, gorgeous girl.' She bent and rubbed

Freya's ears, then laughed as the dog nuzzled her, making her lose her balance. 'Hey. Hey. Yes. I know you love me already.' Now sprawled on the floor, she scrubbed Freya's fur and got face-licks in return. 'Hey! Yes, yes.'

'Freya,' Matthieu snapped and the dog stopped licking and sat completely still, looking up ador-ingly at Matthieu.

Rachel hauled herself upright and sat on the ground, recovering from near death by licking. 'I didn't realise both dogs and bitches pull the sleds.'

'Huskies are bred for speed and agility. Gen-der doesn't come into it. The clever ones go at the front to lead. Freya's a leader.' He smiled as the dog put her paw on Rachel's knee and cocked her head to one side. 'She has very good taste.'

'She just wants a cuddle.' Once again, she was suffused with heat at his words. He gave a lot of compliments and she wasn't sure how to take them. She grabbed the chance to deflect as Freya tugged at Rachel's coat sleeve. 'I think she wants me to come with her.'

Sure enough, Freya led her outside to the sled. 'Okay, so how does this work?'

Matthieu started to clip the dogs on to har-nesses at the front of the sled. They were so clever they knew exactly which order they were to line up in and where to stand. Except Odin, who kept wandering off, only to be called back by Matthieu who never lost his patience. 'You sit on the sled and I stand on the back to steer.'

The fleeting image of them both wrapped up under the rug dissolved as quickly as the spike of desire. 'Why do you need me?'

He motioned for her to sit, pulled the rug over her legs and then gave her the bag to hold. 'You have the most important job. Some of these packages could be fragile and are probably very expensive. I don't want them to fall off and break.'

'Noted. I'll keep tight hold.' She knew he was making up an excuse to distract her from the photo. They both did, but she went with it because…huskies.

And because… Matthieu, she had to admit. How could she not like a man who loved dogs?

David didn't like pets at all.

She really needed to stop thinking about the man who had destroyed her heart and her faith in love.

Matthieu did the click-whistle thing again and the dogs started to run. And…wow!

Just, wow.

The sled breezed across the snow so quickly it almost stripped her breath. The terrain had looked to be all downhill, but it actually undulated in a gradual slow descent. She kept a tight hold on the bag with one hand and a hold on her beanie with the other and the whole time she grinned and screamed in delight.

All too soon, they came to a stop in a chocolate box village with a little square flanked with ancient plane trees and grey stone buildings; she could see a *tabac*, a post office, a greengrocer, a *boulangerie* and a bar on the corner. The bar was bustling with wrapped-up customers sitting outside, beneath fairy lights and heaters.

Matthieu stepped off his spot behind her, anchored the sled in the snow, petted all the dogs, then came over to her. 'Did you have fun?'

'The best. Wow. That was amazing.'

'You look…elated.'

'I didn't think they'd go so fast.' Heart still pounding, she took out her phone and snapped a couple of photos of the dogs.

'Quick, let's take another.' He grabbed her phone and took a picture of her on the sled. 'Smile, Rachel.'

'My face hurts with all the smiling. The dogs, the sled…this place.' *You.* He looked adorable all wrapped up in his scarf and hat with a nose pink from the cold. Her heart stuttered. He really was an extraordinary man to be doing this for her.

But it was one thing to think someone was adorable and another altogether to act on those feelings.

She looked away and started to get out of the sled.

'Wait.' He crouched next to her, cuddled in and

took a snap of them together, cheek to cheek. 'Put that on the internet. That'll show him.'

Matthieu's skin against hers sent shivers of need spiralling through her, but the mention of her ex was enough to chase them away. 'Don't be silly. He won't care.'

'But you do.'

'I do not.' She grabbed for her phone, but he held it away, laughing. His laugh curled around her, making her laugh, too, when once she would have cried over her failed relationship. But, truthfully, she drank him in: his smiling face and kind eyes, his fun-loving streak, his carefree nature. To look for the fun in things was infectious and liberating and so new to her that, after a lifetime of running away from pain, of working so hard and applying her serious work ethic to every aspect of her life, she wanted to chase that fun so hard.

'Honestly, Rachel, you shouldn't give a damn what he thinks.' Matthieu held her gaze. He was close enough she could smell his scent. To see the snowflake crystals land on his nose and upper lip and melt clean away on contact. He really did have the most gorgeous mouth… 'And he's a crazy fool to have let you go.'

Especially when he said things like that. In that French accent that almost brought her to her knees. If she hadn't already been sitting down…

'He didn't let me go. He dumped me at the altar.' Damn. She couldn't believe she'd just admitted that to him. Words had just tumbled out, again. Now he was going to think she was dump-worthy. Instead of kiss-worthy.

Did she want to be kiss-worthy to Matthieu?

But he blinked, his arm still outstretched, his expression one of shock and anger. 'He did... *what*?'

Uh-uh. This was exactly why she kept her thoughts and feelings to herself. So she wouldn't have to relive her most embarrassing and hurtful moments. But she'd started, so she had to tell him the rest. 'He told his best friend to let me know he was sorry, but he couldn't marry me. He said I was too... I was too...'

'Too...? What?' Matthieu encouraged her with his eyes to continue, but she could also see his ire growing, too, on her behalf. His expression of support was like a sucker-punch of heat to her chest.

'Hard to get to know...we'd been going out for two bloody years and now he decides he doesn't know me? I'm cold, apparently. Aloof.'

And she'd tried to be that ever since. Doubled down on it. Keeping everyone at arm's length the way she'd learnt growing up, because that way she wouldn't get hurt again. But Matthieu...he was sorely testing her resolve.

'He actually said that? You? Dr Blow-Up? Is-la's advocate? Lover of huskies? Cold?' Matthieu smiled and shook his head. 'Private, yes. And there's nothing wrong with that. Not everyone wants to live their lives on social media. Independent, definitely. But clearly, he hasn't seen you stand up for an injured child or roll on the floor with a puppy. Even so…even if he thought those things of you, to leave you at a church on your wedding day is unforgivable.'

'I hadn't seen it coming, so it was a shock. Sure, we were in a routine, but he called it a rut, like a weight on his shoulders he couldn't carry any more. He said I was too closed off, but I tried, I really tried to be part of a couple. I'm just not one to wear my heart on my sleeve and say how I'm feeling, it's just not who I am.'

'Can I ask…' he pulled an apologetic face '…why would he propose to you if he didn't think he knew you?'

Her cheeks heated. She swallowed. *God,* this was embarrassing. 'I asked him.'

'Ah.'

'Yes. *Ah.* It was leap year. And I thought it was what he wanted. Turns out it was, just not with me.'

Matthieu groaned. 'He's crazy.'

'I must be to have proposed, right? We were on holiday in Crete and it had been a good day; we'd swum in the sea, done some sightseeing— nothing mind-blowing, but it had been easy, you know? Everything seemed to slot into place. At least, I thought it had. I was content.'

After seeing her parents' passion turn to hate she'd steered away from extreme emotions. Hadn't wanted or looked for an all-consuming big love because she knew how that ended.

'I said it would be nice if every day was like this and he agreed. And then I said, "So marry me, David."'

'That would have taken some guts, Rachel.'

She laughed. 'On paper he was perfect. Steady and reliable and the opposite of what I'd grown up with. I wanted stability, I guess, and thought he'd give me that. I felt like I belonged, finally. That I was part of something that wasn't just my team of one. Something...content.'

'What did he say when you proposed?'

'He looked at me open-mouthed for a few moments, making me feel like an idiot, and then eventually nodded. I'd thought it was the surprise that made him hesitate, but apparently he'd been too worried to say no in case I got upset.'

'Leaving you at the altar isn't upsetting?'

'He said he'd been trying to tell me for weeks, but thought that he might just have pre-wedding jitters. He realised on the day that he couldn't go through with it. And now I'm seeing pictures of him and Vicky. Our friend. Engaged.'

'You know her, too?'

'She was in our friendship group. More my friend than his, or so I thought. Problem was, we worked together and shared the same friends and colleagues…when you work weird shifts it's hard to make friends outside work and you just sort of form a team who you socialise with, too.' That's what she'd hoped for, anyway. 'So, everyone we knew, knew about what had happened. That he didn't want me. That I wasn't good enough. Just not…enough for him.'

She laughed, but it was empty, wondering why the hell she was telling this guy all about the previous guy who'd discarded her. 'The two weeks we were supposed to be on honeymoon we spent separating our things and looking for a place for him to move into, speaking only through text messages. I couldn't bring myself to talk to him. I had nothing to say.'

'God, Rachel, that's cruel.' Matthieu's gaze had softened. He was looking at her as if none of this made sense.

That made two of them. At least, it hadn't made any sense to her at the time, but now she was starting to see that her tendency to keep things close to her chest could be seen as aloof and cold. The way she always told everyone she was fine didn't invite anyone in. In fact, Matthieu had said as much on that first morning and opened her eyes to how she came across to other people.

Why she was baring her soul to him like this she didn't know, except that the words were pouring out of her and he was interested, seemed almost invested.

Although she was probably scaring him off.

'We still worked in the same department most days and it was stifling. I love my job. I live for my work and I got to the point where I didn't want to go in. That's when I knew I had to leave. And that's why I came here. I needed to get away from it all.'

She blew out the pain of embarrassment and hurt. Her breath plumed in the cold air, mingling with Matthieu's. She watched as the vapour wisps curled together and then faded into nothing right in front of them. Gone. She sent all her sadness that, way too, out into the atmosphere to disappear. Gone. All the hurt from that day. Gone.

'You have some unfinished business, then?' he said.

'No. God, no. David knows what I think of him.' The love she'd felt for him had turned into something a lot uglier and messier. But now she just didn't want to think about her ex at all.

Matthieu laughed. Actually laughed. 'Poor guy.'

And for the first time in what felt like for ever, Rachel gave a hearty laugh, too. 'He's probably quaking in his boots, waiting for me to unleash.'

'Don't give him the satisfaction.'

'I have no plans to. I just want to forget him. Forget her. Forget them.' Surprisingly, after talking about it, her chest felt lighter. Her heart felt lighter. She knew she had a lot more work to do, but right now she was free from five months' worth of heartache. She'd escaped Leeds and all those repressed emotions that she'd swallowed so she wouldn't blow up in front of her friends... and here she could breathe and be free. She had everything to look forward to.

The thirty years' worth of another kind of heartache was going to take a bit longer to breathe out—another time.

Heck, she was in France with a gorgeous man and six adorable dogs. Suddenly, she was acutely aware of the press of Matthieu's thigh against hers, of the rise and fall of his chest. Of his strength and heat.

'You know what? To hell with all that. It's all in the past.' She was determined to let it stay there. 'Look at me. I'm here, on a freaking husky sled. It's magical. Beautiful. Wonderful. I'm not going to let anyone ruin this moment. But please give me the phone, my whole life's in there.'

'Only if you promise to upload that photo of us to that stupid website. Show him that you've moved on. A picture with a sexy Frenchman might help, yes?' Matthieu made a pretence of preening.

'Sexy?' She laughed. 'You have one seriously big ego, Matthieu LeFevre.'

'And...? What's the problem?' He winked, getting up to give each of the dogs a treat. Walking along the line, then back to the sled. 'I haven't had any complaints so far.'

'Honestly…' she tutted, playing along. 'I bet *most* women hang off every word you say.' She emphasised most, making the point that she wouldn't be one of them.

'It's a drag…but…yes.' His grin stretched. 'Seriously, who could keep away from me and six gorgeous huskies?' He nuzzled Odin's neck and fluttered his eyelashes at her. 'Look at this one. How could you resist those puppy eyes?'

'You use your dogs to score dates?' Giggling, she bugged her eyes back at him in mock horror. 'Matthieu, I'm shocked.'

'Actually, I've only just thought about it. But it's an excellent idea. Thanks for the tip.'

'Oh, you know me. Such a successful love life. Any time you want advice, I'm…your…girl.'

Her words slowed as she realised Matthieu's grin had slipped. He had completely stilled and was looking at her with such sexual hunger it made her insides liquid. And she knew, she just *knew* he'd brought her here on the sled because he wanted to make her happy. And that made him the sexiest man she'd ever met.

Their gazes tangled and the atmosphere seemed to charge with a delicious sexual tension.

He reached a gloved palm to her cheek and stroked her skin. She curled into his touch, wanting and wishing to press her mouth to his. To press her body against his.

'Dr Tait, has anyone ever told you how pretty you are when you smile?'

Her throat worked, but she wasn't sure she could find words.

'No,' she managed. 'Never.'

He ran a finger over her lip, making her shiver with anticipation. 'Beautiful.'

'You know that line we talked about?' She barely recognised her own voice, it was so sex-fuelled and cracked with need.

'The other day?' His eyes twinkled and he twisted his whole body to face her. 'Yes.'

She couldn't believe she was saying this, but she had to. 'Do you ever cross it on a personal level?'

His other palm cupped her cheek and he encouraged her to stand up. 'I haven't, to date.'

'You want to make an exception?' she said. This was the kicker...had what she told him put him off?

His face inched closer, she could see snow-flakes on his eyelashes and that made her heart melt just a bit more. 'Will it make things awkward, Rachel?'

'I don't know.' She pressed her hand to his cheek, too. 'Probably.'

'This is just to get your ex back, yes? Get him out of your system?' The way he looked at her told her that was an excuse, not a reason. He wanted this as much as she did. His eyes had become very serious indeed and blazed with heat.

'I don't know. I just... I just have to...' *Kiss you.*

'Say it, Rachel. Tell me what you want.'

*Ray Shell. Ray Shell.* Way to make an ice queen melt.

But this was exactly what she couldn't do. Sure, in her working life she could command the whole ER to do her bidding. But this...? Asking for things she wanted? How many times had she done that growing up and been ignored? To the point she'd learnt not to ask at all.

But it was clear he wasn't going to respond until she said the words. What was the worst that could happen? She'd already been rejected in the worst possible way. All Matthieu could do was walk away and, judging by the way he was looking at her, she didn't think he'd do that right now. 'I want to kiss you, Matthieu.'

'The feeling is very, *very* mutual.' He stepped closer until his body pressed against hers.

'Are you sure, after everything I just told you?'

'Why would that put me off? You were being honest. I like that.' He pressed her against the trunk of an ancient plane tree, caught her bottom lip between his teeth and smiled. 'Very cold. But heating up nicely.'

Then he slid his mouth over hers.

# CHAPTER NINE

OH, SHE WAS COLD, all right.

But not in the way her ex had meant. Her lips were like ice from the whip of freezing air. Her cheeks were so cold he felt it through his gloves.

But her mouth… God, her mouth was hot and wet and divine.

She tasted of fresh snow mixed with the Chablis she'd been drinking earlier, of renewal and excitement, and he felt it emanating through her.

She tasted, quite simply, exquisite. But she was holding back…wanting it, but hesitant. Keeping herself in control, apart in some way. Knowing her the way he did, she was probably telling herself it was just *fine*.

Which made him smile inside. Because he knew she was a whole lot more than fine right now. He also knew this was probably the most insane thing he'd ever done, because Rachel had just come out of a relationship that had broken her heart. She needed to heal. Needed more than he could give her. But, like her, he just wanted one kiss. One taste. If nothing else than to erase the spectre of her ex from her head.

No, if nothing else…just to taste her. Over and over.

He pulled away slightly and looked at her. Her eyes were wide open, but her dark pupils were huge and misted. He laughed, kissed her cheek, her nose, then one eyelid and the other, forcing them closed, hoping she'd relax. 'You are exquisite, Rachel.'

'Say it again.' Eyes still closed, she curled into his palm on her cheek. 'Say my name.'

'Rachel.' He licked her bottom lip. Then her top one. *Je veux t'embrasser partout,*' he whispered into her mouth.

'Kiss me all over? *God*, Matthieu…' He saw the moment she finally let herself fall. Her eyes had shuttered closed, but he could see the heat and desire in her features, in the pink stain on her cheeks, the way she tilted her head. The puckering of those lips, the swallow in her throat.

The kiss deepened and he felt her soften against him as if she was breathing out and finally letting the control slip. She circled her hands round his shoulders and tugged him closer until he could feel the press of her breasts against his chest. The hitch of her breathing.

As her tongue slid into his mouth fresh arousal shot through him, hot and tight. Deep in his belly. Hard in his groin. Prickling over his skin and under his skin, in his chest, in his bones. He felt the need for her *everywhere*.

He'd had a glimpse of the real Rachel Tait, the heart of her, and now he wanted to see through to her core. He wanted her open, he wanted her falling apart with him rocking deep inside her.

'Matthieu. I need…this.' She moaned and her hands cupped his backside, tugging him closer and closer.

Whoever said this woman was cold had absolutely no idea. She just needed time and the right kind of kissing.

*Woof! Woof!*

The dogs! *Damn.*

The barking brought him crash-landing back to reality.

They were in his village—everyone knew him. He'd always kept his liaisons out of their glare— mainly to protect his mother—but now the local gossip machine would whirr into action.

Hell, he half expected a round of applause from the crowd over at the bar, until he realised they were hidden by the tree trunk.

He tugged away from her, reluctant to let her go now she'd finally opened up enough for a kiss, however brief, but knowing it was the right thing to do.

Desire had made him rash, letting his body lead. But they'd been reckless kissing out here. Kissing at all. Now he had to let things cool.

She looked thoroughly dazed and thoroughly kissed. He pushed a stray lock of hair back under her beanie and couldn't stop the smile. 'Has he gone?'

'Who?' She smiled back up at him, but he could feel her trembling against him. He was shaken up, too. He'd never had a kiss like that. Full, giving, open.

'We should probably head back, but let's drop the bag off to Natalie first,' he said. Then he gave the dogs another treat and tied the sled off on the tree trunk.

Maybe real life would set his brain straight.

But, of course, it didn't. All he could think about was the way she'd looked at him when he'd licked her bottom lip—as if she wanted to eat him. He'd never seen a woman so hungry for a kiss. For *his* kiss.

He tried to bury those thoughts as they talked with Natalie. And he wondered if Rachel was thinking the same...that it had been a mistake. She was gracious and friendly with Natalie. Quiet on the ride home, no screeching at the speed, no huge smiles.

She seemed to have turned in on herself—not actively blocking him or pushing him away, but not allowing him in either—and she wasn't pursuing any deeper conversation than polite, which he should have been grateful for, because he didn't want deep. Sure, he knew the value of community and friendship, but anything more intimate? He'd never been able to go there. And wasn't about to start.

Once the dogs had been fed, watered and put back into their kennels. she hugged her arms round her chest. 'I should go. It's late.'

He secured Odin's kennel, then turned to her. 'Let me walk you back to your chalet.'

'I'm fine—' She smiled, rolled her eyes, then corrected herself. 'I mean… I know my way.'

He couldn't read her. Didn't know what she was thinking.

The last thing he wanted was to have to sec-ond-guess someone else. He'd done that all his life with his mother: watching her moods, interpret-ing her expressions, assessing, guarding, prepar-ing himself for whatever she was going to throw at him, which was always unpredictable. What he needed was transparent. What he liked was easy.

'Are you okay, Rachel? You haven't said much since…the village.'

'It's been a long time since I did anything like that.' She sighed. 'And I'm naturally a quiet per-son. I do a lot of thinking and not so much talk-ing. But the thing is, I need my space. I need to— Look, Matthieu, I'm not looking for a rela-tionship right now.'

'Of course. Me neither.' Rachel was a special woman and he was intrigued and turned on by her. But that was where it had to stop. He nodded his assent, then kissed both of her cheeks in as platonic a way as he could muster. 'Goodnight, Rachel.'

She squeezed his hand. 'Thank you for the adventure. It was a lot of fun.'

'No problem. I enjoyed it, too. Very much.' He nodded then turned away.

Truth was, Matt knew it was a lot more than fun. But, no matter what his sensible brain was telling him, he ached to do it again.


Rachel closed the front door of her chalet and leaned back against the wood, her heart jittering and her insides tightening at the memory of his mouth on hers. Had she just made another of her catastrophic mistakes?

Probably. But it had been one of her better ones. Her best worst mistake?

'Oh, God.' She put her head in her hands, her cheeks burning at the mortification and wonder of it. She'd kissed him. She couldn't stop the giggle bursting out of her. Since when had she ever giggled?

He'd wanted to kiss her all over.

*Yes, please.* It had been a wonderful kiss, but a crazy idea. It was right they'd agreed not to take it any further.


She had barely slept for reliving his touch, his taste, and she got up the next morning feeling two-parts groggy and one-part still excited.

Had she ever thought about David like this? Lain awake and yearned for him? Overly excited at the prospect of seeing him again? She didn't think so, couldn't remember ever having this washing machine churn in her stomach. Their relationship had always been just, well... nice enough, satisfactory. Their sex life had been perfunctory and she'd been okay with that, not expecting or wanting big passion like her parents.

David had been serious, like her. Practical, like her. Then he'd gone and fallen hopelessly in love with someone else. It didn't seem fair that he got to do the dumping *and* the falling in love.

A long day off stretched before her.

She had made some breakfast, read her emails, then looked round her little chalet for something to do. She'd felt on edge, jittery, as if she needed some serious exercise to get rid of the excess energy coursing through her.

She couldn't just sit around here replaying that kiss, so she went out to see the dogs, gave them each a pat and cuddle and found some treats that she sneaked in to them. Then she wandered through the resort, looked in the high-end shops at things she didn't want to buy. Had a coffee and pastry in a cafe. Then... What to do?

Normally she'd have read a book, but today restlessness ate at her until she couldn't take it any longer. She couldn't wait until four o'clock before she did some exercise, she needed to do some now.

She rushed back to her chalet, dressed for skiing, then climbed on to the chairlift, pausing to tell the liftie, 'In case anyone asks, I'm going up to the top trails. I have my personal locator beacon in case of emergency and I'll be back for the staff ski session at four.'

He saluted as the chairlift cranked up speed. 'Got you, Doc. Have fun.'

'I will!' Then she clutched the safety bar, remembering, too late, the headphones that she'd last seen on the dining table in her chalet.

*Looks like I'm going to have to listen to my thoughts, then.*

Not great. The last thing she needed was to relive that kiss all over again.

She set off along a route the group had skied the other day, but things were different today; the sky was filled with clouds, the visibility wasn't as good, the snow was hard and icy. She knew she'd have to keep her wits about her.

*Cold. Aloof.*
*Ray Shell.*
*Ice Queen.*
*Lover of huskies.*
*Isla's advocate.*
*Kisser of Matthieu.*
*Ray Shell.*

It started to snow, thick white flakes falling fast

all around her. She skied through them, catching them on her tongue and laughing. Glad to be so free and having some space and time on her own and, yet, strangely alone. She'd come to enjoy skiing in a group, the laughter and challenges and just the…friendship. Should she have waited until four o'clock? Should she have invited someone to come with her? Zoe? Matthieu?

They all seemed to like her, too, even though she kept them all at a distance by design.

What had she missed by being so closed off? Should she talk more? Was that the problem? Is that what people in successful relationships did? They talked. Not argued like her parents. They communicated. Could she do that? Apparently not enough, as far as David was concerned. Even Matthieu had mentioned her silence last night.

After that kiss.

*Shoot!* Her foot skidded on the ice and she careened sideways, her body twisting until she was facing directly down the mountain. It was steep. But she could manage. She let the momentum take her straight down until she gathered enough control to put pressure on her inner ski and turn swiftly and in control.

Her heart slowed. Good. Right. No more Matthieu thoughts because they seemed to sap her attention. The snow was falling faster now, coating the track with fresh powder, shrouding her in a cloak of white.

She skied across the mountain to a trail she hadn't seen before. It had a gentle descent, meandering through the trees, and looked to be heading towards the resort buildings. She took it, easing her way down a picturesque track flanked by pine trees.

It reminded her of last night on the sled. The cute dogs with quaint names.

And then the kiss.

It had been so good to be in Matthieu's arms. She'd felt as if she'd come home, so wanted. Desired. He'd pushed her to open up and she'd felt so free. More, he'd seen her as someone more than a jilted woman. More than a doctor. And he'd treated her with such care.

She'd wavered about him walking her home. Debated in her head about inviting him in to her chalet. She hadn't known what to do, so she'd panicked—

*Ugh.* Her foot struck something hard and suddenly she was flying through the air.

*No!* She tried to right herself, but landed hard and off balance, the impact on slippery ice flinging her forward, her left ski breaking loose and skittering to the edge of the mountain...disappearing over the edge...

She watched it go as she tumbled over and over, hitting small rocks, the impacted snow. She couldn't stop...didn't stop, in free fall down the deceptively steep hill, putting one hand out

to slow her fall, one hand on her helmet to protect her head. There were trees in front of her,
trees everywhere, and she was flying, tumbling
towards them. Too fast.

*Please. Stop. Please.*

She held her breath, closed her eyes. Braced
for impact, hoping this would be survivable, but
knowing there was a chance it wouldn't be. Isla's
little impassive face flittered through her mind,
then Odin's. Then Matthieu's.

*Matthieu, I'm sorry...*

Suddenly she came to a crashing halt as her
back collided hard with a tree trunk. For a few
moments she lay there dazed, unsure which way
was up. Numb to everything apart from the fact
she was still alive.

*Stupid. Stupid. Stupid.*

A searing pain radiated up her right leg. Her
back stung from the impact. She sat up, a little dizzy and shocked at how quickly things had
turned bad.

*Mooning over a man.*

'Get up. Get up and go home, girl,' she told herself as adrenalin kicked in, making her more alert,
but shaky. 'Get up, already.' She hauled herself
upright and tugged up her salopettes. Her right
knee was red and raw and swelling up. *Damn.*

What to do? More to the point, where was she?
The falling snow was so thick it felt as if she was

in a cloud, unable to see much beyond her outstretched hand.

She looked around, trying to get her bearings. There was no track here, she'd skidded off it, leaving a trail of tiny, fluffy snowballs and grit in her wake. Her one ski was cracked, but still attached to her boot. She flicked it off. One ski was no use. Hopping all the way back down the mountain would take hours and she'd risk hypothermia, but it was her only option. But which way? Where was the track?

If she set off the locator beacon, she'd bring the whole search and rescue team out to her... she didn't need that. They didn't need that...this wasn't a real emergency. She was just a little... dazed. Perhaps a bit lost. In a bit of pain.

A lot of pain.

She just needed to know where she was. She took out her phone to look at the GPS map. The screen was cracked. No signal. She peered closer. All she could see were a few jagged coloured lines. She jabbed at the screen—no response. The fall must have broken it.

*Hell.*

She remembered veering off the track further up, so she'd walk back up and find it. That would be the only way she'd get her bearings. *Right. A plan. Good.*

She peered up the hill, which seemed a lot steeper than she'd originally thought. A lot of up. But that was the only way she'd find her way home.

Back to Matthieu.

Her stomach flipped. Matthieu.

Yes. Thinking about him gave her the impetus to move. She didn't know where she was, but she was pretty certain up was the way to go. Yes. That's where she'd go.

Having retrieved, thankfully, both her poles, she put herself perpendicular to the mountain and kick-stepped and limped her way up the ice, inch by inch, using the poles as walking sticks until she reached the point where she thought her ski and backpack had flown over the edge. There, below, a pink-tipped ski stuck out of the snow and her backpack was further down.

There was no way she'd get down there, so it was back towards the trail.

*Come on, girl. You've got this.*

As the ascent levelled out, she hopped slowly through the ever-falling snow until she found something that resembled the track—she just couldn't see where it led and it was completely deserted. But she set her stall on the resort being eastwards and downwards, so started to trudge, trying to ignore the pain in her back and her leg.

She sang. 'Living on a Prayer'. 'Stairway to Heaven'. 'Bohemian Rhapsody'. 'Eye of the Tiger'. 'Total Eclipse of the Heart'.

Then she ran out of songs and energy.

*No point bringing snacks if they're in a back-pack out of reach. Just need a rest.*

Tired and thirsty, she slumped down on to the snow and sat for a few moments, easing the ache in her back. Taking a breath. Everything hurt now: her lungs, her back, her knee, her head. Exhaustion swamped her.

Surely it couldn't be too far? It wasn't dark yet, although the visibility was still very poor.

It would have been good to have someone with her right now. They could have laughed this whole episode off, then trudge-hopped down to the resort for après-ski. That would have taken her mind off the pain and the cold that seeped through her salopettes and under her skin.

*If I ever get out of here alive, I'm going to make sure I have more fun.*

She would keep on kissing Matthieu.

She would invite him in. Yes. She'd invite him in. Because to deny herself some pleasure of the Matthieu variety had been pretty darned stupid. He hadn't been asking for for ever, he'd just asked to walk her home. Instead of curling into her shell, instead of not taking a risk, she should have said, *hell, yes!*

The thought of kissing Matthieu gave her an incentive to carry on. She forced herself to stand up again and started walking when something caught her eye. A silver bird shimmered above her in a brief break in the clouds. She lifted her hand to shield her eyes. It wasn't a bird. Was it a bird?

Had she hit her head? Her back hurt with every step, but she was convinced it was just bruised. She knew she hadn't hit her head. She looked skywards again. The silver bird had disappeared.

She looked ahead of her and realised the path was no longer there. Panic wormed into her gut. She was lost and she was all alone.

Again.

# CHAPTER TEN

'SHE'S ABOUT FIFTY metres off Heaven's Gate. Just past the copse, to the left. Looks like she's lost her skis.' Cody expertly landed the drone and looked over at Matt, grimacing. 'She doesn't look in great shape.'

'Let's go get her,' Matt snapped at his colleague and tried to control the emotions swirling inside him. 'Come on, man. Hurry up.'

'On it.' Cody jumped on to the back of the evac snowmobile as Matt gunned the engine, then they sped off up the mountain towards the Heaven's Gate track.

The returning cloud cover had hit fifteen-hundred metres and as they climbed to the higher altitude it was like riding through soup. What the hell had she been doing skiing out here in this weather? They'd closed the ski fields an hour ago because the conditions were so dangerous. His gut clenched as he fought back rising concern. What if something bad had happened to her? What was he going to find up there on the mountain?

*God, no. Please.*

He slammed thoughts of that day two years ago. Whatever he found, he'd deal with it. And deal with the fallout later.

Weird thing was, he'd done countless evacs like this and not once had he had this tight panic in his gut. Memories of last night's kiss added heat to it.

Yes. He was a mess.

He peered through the falling flakes. Everything was whited out. 'Can you see anything?' he called to Cody.

'Literally nothing. Visibility's probably five metres, if we're lucky.'

They rode along the track to the end. Nothing. Not even footprints. Everything was covered in fresh snow.

'Damn it.' Matt hit the handlebar with his palm. 'Let's circle round and try again.'

They did another loop and his heart dimmed like the fading daylight. She wasn't here. 'One more go-round? Then we'll widen the search.'

'Wait. There. There!' Cody nudged him and pointed to their right. 'Is that her? Can you see something pink?'

Matt willed his eyes to focus. Was there something?

A movement caught his eye. He steered closer. Something…? Her ski jacket?

'Rachel? Rachel!' he shouted into the blinding whiteness.

They sat in silence, craning their necks to listen. Nothing.

'Rachel?'

Nothing.

And then…

'Matthieu?' Faint. 'Matthieu?'

All the air whooshed out of his lungs and his body relaxed. She was talking—that had to be a good sign. 'Hold on! We're coming to get you.'

He jumped off the snowmobile and ran towards a bundle on the ground.

*Please be okay. Please be okay.*

Memories of another day, another woman swamped him. That time he hadn't been so lucky.

She was slumped over, cheeks pink with cold, lips a funny shade of grey. 'Rachel. Rachel.'

'Matthieu?' She started to sit up, but slumped back down again. 'Oh.'

The panic had hitched a ride with all the air from Matt's lungs, replaced by relief and an overwhelming feeling of…what, he wasn't sure. All he knew was that he was beyond glad to have found her. He managed to control himself enough not to wrap her in his arms in front of Cody. Instead, he crouched down to assess her. She looked frozen through, but was conscious, so that was something. 'Hey there. What's happened?'

Her forehead scrunched into a frown, but there was a brittle, false brightness in her voice. 'I was…exploring.'

'And how was that going for you?' He gestured to their environs. 'Making your own path down, instead of following a perfectly decent one just a few metres over there?'

'Ah, that's where it is.' She blinked and smiled weakly. 'I like making my own path, right? You know that.'

So, they were going to play the *pretend everything's okay* game. Frustration swelled in his chest, tingeing the initial relief that they'd found her alive. He wanted to shake her and kiss her at the same time. Then he remembered she'd insisted on having space. He edged away a little, not wanting to overwhelm her. 'Where are your skis?'

'One went over the mountainside when I took a bit of a tumble and I'm sensible enough not to go down a sheer cliff to retrieve it. I couldn't manage to ski without it and I couldn't carry the other one. So, I'm walking. I was walking, but...' She stretched her leg out and grimaced. She'd taken her boot off for some reason.

'What's happened to your leg?'

'Oh, it's probably nothing.' Although she wasn't able to hide the wince. 'I just bent it a bit in the tumble. It'll be fine. I've just been putting ice on it while I rested for a minute.'

'You must be totally freezing, then.'

'It is a bit chilly. Thank goodness for ski wear.' She was at least able to answer him coherently. But the risk of hypothermia was increasing the longer they stayed up here. She hugged her jacket close to her. 'Um… Can I hitch a ride down?'

'Rachel, we came to get you,' he explained, as gently as he could. 'I think you might have some hypothermia.' Confusion was a symptom.

Although, really, he was the mixed-up person here. Relieved and frustrated and just plain glad to see her. He fought the desire to stroke her cheek, knowing she wouldn't want such a display in front of one of their work colleagues. Knowing it was better for both of them if they stuck to last night's agreement. 'We thought you might be lost. We closed the ski field ages ago because the conditions quickly deteriorated and it was too dangerous to be up the mountain. Didn't you hear the siren?'

'I was singing.' As if that was the most natural thing to do in a snowstorm.

'Of course you were.' He imagined her bobbing her head and singing out of tune like the other day and smiled. 'We put up a drone and saw you wandering up here.'

'A drone? Oh. Yes. Of course. The bird.' For a moment she pressed her lips together and he could have sworn he saw tears swim in her eyes, but if they were, she soon blinked them away. 'Were you looking for me? You didn't have to, I'm fine.'

'So why are you sitting down in the snow in the middle of nowhere?'

'I heard you calling so I stopped walking. If

you're waiting…or hoping, for someone to find you, the most important thing is to stay where you are. I heard the engine and then your voices and stayed put.'

'Good. But what about your locator beacon? Why didn't you use it?'

'I was just about to.' She shrugged and shivered. 'But then you appeared, as if I'd conjured you up.'

Now it was his turn to press his lips together, although it was more a case of trying not to curse at her. Setting off the beacon would have brought them to her earlier. But he knew hypothermia slowed thought processes, too. He wrapped her in a thermal blanket. 'Let's get you on to the snowmobile.'

'Yes, please.' She went to stand, but grimaced and closed her eyes. Her hand went to her back and she rubbed. He watched as she literally smoothed her expression from one of pain to one of light-heartedness. 'Just give me a moment.'

'Wait.' He leaned over her, halting her movements. 'Have you hurt your back, too? What's happened?'

'Just a little bump. It's stiffened up since I stopped moving.'

'What about now?' He ran his fingers down her spine, checked her limbs. Checked her neck. But she shook away from him. 'I've just been walking up the mountain, Matthieu. Neither my back or neck are broken, I promise. I can—'

'Cody…give me a hand.' He looped his arm under her armpit and Cody did the same on the other side and they helped her stand. She straightened, then bent, then finally straightened. Pain ran across her features.

He was surprised when she didn't refuse his help and took his outstretched arm to enable her to climb on to the snowmobile. Ice had formed on the strands of hair sticking out from her helmet. He lay her on the stretcher and tucked the silver emergency blanket round her. And then layered up another blanket and tightened the tarp cover over her. 'Warm enough?'

Her eyes had fluttered closed and she gave him a grateful smile. 'I will be now.'

'I promise the first thing I'll do back at base is make you my famous *chocolat chaud*.'

'Yes, please. That sounds perfect.' She didn't open her eyes, but this time her smile was full and genuine. She looked almost peaceful lying there, except for the wince of pain that drew little frown lines on her forehead. He imagined her asleep in his bed. Waking up to her. She was so beautiful. So frustratingly gorgeous.

And so out of reach.

Regardless, his heart gave a little stretch. 'You gave me a fright, Rachel.'

'I'm sorry for worrying you.' Opening her eyes,

she put a hand to his face. 'Thank you for coming to get me.'

'Don't thank me until we've got you back to base.'

Why the hell had she been skiing on her own in these conditions?

But he knew her well enough that she would do what she wanted—she was her own woman and that was what he liked about her. But that independence also came with side-effects. He wasn't sure how to navigate that.

His mother had been all about emotion…dark, tragic, painful emotion that had leached out of her all the time. Tears. Angry outbursts. Highs. Lows.

Rachel was the opposite. She kept it all inside her. It would take a special kind of guy to tease her out of herself, to get her to share. He wondered if he could be that man. If he even wanted to be.

*No.*

Everything in him shied away from deep personal connections. But something about Rachel pierced his own emotional walls. He couldn't reconcile the concern, the raw panic he'd felt when they couldn't find her. Didn't want to care that much for someone again, only to lose them.

But he gently tucked the silver blanket around her some more. Then, without second-guessing himself, he leaned in and pressed a kiss to her forehead. 'You're safe now.'

'I am. I was… I have to admit… I was starting to panic a bit.' She blinked at him, giddiness
swimming in her eyes. 'Thank God for drones.
I love the ski patrol. I love hot chocolate. And I
love you, Matthieu LeFevre.'

What? Matt's chest hurt. He did not know what
to say to that. Because he knew she didn't mean
it and, stupidly, foolishly, he wanted her to. Wondered what it would take for her to actually mean
it, to feel it. Knowing also that she wouldn't let
herself slide into that feeling, not after what she'd
been through with her ex.

'Aww, get a room, you two.' Cody laughed.

'Oh, I love you, too, Cody.' She grinned. 'My
knights in shining salopettes.'

'She's clearly hypothermic and doesn't know
what she's saying.' Matt knew she was just plain
grateful, but he couldn't shake the weird feeling
in his chest that was at once weighty and light.
And it scared the hell out of him. 'Crazy to be out
here on her own. Isn't that right, Rachel?'

She smiled up at him, her eyes a little bit wild.
'I think I got lost.'

'You think…?' He didn't know whether to
laugh or cry.

Then there was nothing left to say as they sped
down to the medical centre.

Rachel wasn't sure which hurt most: the pain in
her bones or the sting of embarrassment at being

the patient and adding to the workload of her colleagues.

'Honestly, please don't fuss. I'm fine,' she told Suzanne as the nurse examined her knee.

'I'm not fussing, I'm assessing. Take these painkillers.' Suzanne handed Rachel a plastic pot of two white tablets and a glass of water, then looked at the bruising blooming across her knee. 'You need a scan of that injury.'

'I know.' Rachel's heart sank at the prospect of time off work. 'I'll sort it out tomorrow. Let's just put a brace on tonight and leave it at that.'

'If you're sure? I'll pop this on, then say goodnight.' Suzanne slipped a black brace over the swollen knee, secured it with Velcro, then waved goodbye.

'Okay. That feels better already.' Rachel hopped down from the gurney and wiggled her toes, half glad she was now alone with Matthieu and yet half anxious. Because, after their kiss last night, everything was muddied.

He'd been by her side the whole time, looking after her, cajoling and being kind, but she could feel tension radiating from him as he'd gradually emotionally retreated from her since they'd arrived at the medical centre.

She imbued her voice with a brightness she didn't feel. 'The support really helps.'

'I'll run you down to the resort on the snowmobile so you can get a proper shoe for the other foot.' Matthieu held her coat out for her to slide her arms in, but kept his distance at the same time. 'Then, I'll drive you to Bourg St Maurice hospital. I'll call ahead and let them know we're on our way.'

'Honestly, not tonight. I just want to get warm and dry and have a rest. The scan can wait until tomorrow.' The pain was so intense she just wanted to lie down and she didn't want to take up any more of Matthieu's time. 'It won't affect the management plan to wait until the morning.'

He frowned. 'Surely the sooner you get it fixed the better?'

'Tomorrow will be fine. I'll just go soak in my spa bath.'

'On your own?'

'Matthieu?' That was unexpected. Her eyes darted from him to Suzanne's disappearing form. Had she heard? Was he really suggesting…?

He saw her reaction and then his eyes misted. 'I mean, you shouldn't be on your own.'

'I'll be okay. The painkillers should kick in soon.' But thoughts of her and Matthieu relaxing in the spa bath had taken centre-stage in her brain. Her knight in lashings of bubble bath, although a happier Matthieu than this withdrawn one in front of her.

He huffed out a breath. For some reason his emotional distance was sliding into frustration. 'Rachel, you're obviously in a lot of pain. I can't allow you to be on your own when you're like this. What if you have an emergency during the night? Internal bleeding?' He stared at her. 'Would you allow someone to be on their own... like this?' He gesticulated to her knee and then her back.

'There's no internal bleeding. I'm quite sure of that.'

'You have X-ray eyes?'

'No. But—' She started to hop, but a searing pain in her back made her stop. Take a breath. Grip the side of the gurney.

'You expect to be able to do everything for yourself when you can't even walk a few steps?'

'I'll manage. I'm strong.' She could do this on her own. She'd managed well enough on her own for most of her life. She didn't need help.

He opened the door and she hopped through it, biting her lip against the pain. 'Go on, then.'

'Okay.' If he didn't believe in her, then she would show him she could do this.

She took a deep breath and put her weight on her foot. Then stopped. Used her good leg to lead instead. But she didn't get further than the doorway before she had to stop. She leaned against the doorjamb, looking at the distance that stretched between her and the chairlift. This morning she could have done it in a few strides without even thinking, now it was an interminable distance.

It wasn't just her knee and her back, it felt as if

everything hurt and as if someone had siphoned every ounce of energy from her body. She'd spent everything she had climbing back up that hill. Basically, she was exhausted. Done.

And from a medical perspective she shouldn't really use her bad leg, so perhaps an evening with help would allow her to rest and start to heal. She looked up to see him watching her with a stony expression, and barely had the energy to form words. 'Okay, you have a point, I may need some help for tonight. But where do you expect me to go?'

'Well done. I know it would have cost you a lot to say that.' He pressed his lips together as he thought. 'I'll call Suzanne. You could stay at hers.'

He tapped his phone, spoke, then clicked off and shook his head. 'She's unavailable tonight. I'll call Zoe.'

He clearly didn't want to offer his place and she couldn't blame him after the weirdness that followed the kiss. And she sure as hell wasn't going to suggest it and risk his rejection.

So much for all those promises she'd made to herself on the mountain. *She would let him in. She'd do more kissing. Great.* She hadn't accounted for *him* not wanting more kissing.

And yet, why hadn't it? It wasn't as if she had a slew of men wanting her.

But there'd been a connection between them.

He shook his head again and finished the call.

'She's busy, too. There's nothing for it. You'll have to stay with me.' He didn't look happy about the prospect.

'I'm sure I'll be okay in my own place—'

'Rachel. No.' He raised his hand the way she'd done to quieten Bianca. It worked. She closed her mouth. 'I'll send Fred over to get some of your things. My place is bigger; I have three bedrooms, unlike your one-bedroomed chalet. We'll be able to give each other the space we need.'

Space? Judging by the way he was looking at her, she'd clearly upset him. How could she fix it? Her parents would have shouted at each other. David would have slunk away and sulked...as would she in days past.

But Matthieu? He pushed her to open up. Showing her there could be another way. Making her want to find that way.

Inviting someone in meant you accepted them, warts and all. It also meant talking instead of arguing. Understanding instead of jumping to conclusions.

He slid an arm under her shoulders to steady her as she hopped and she said, 'Matthieu, are you angry with me?'

He breathed out. 'To be honest, Rachel, I don't know.'

'Okay.' An ache swirled into her chest. 'Is it because I won't get the scan tonight? Because I fell? Because I went skiing on my own? Or am I missing something?'

'Because…' He stopped walking and stared at her, as if trying to weigh up what to say. Eventually, he shook his head in what looked like defeat and exasperation. 'Because you got hurt.'

'You're cross because I fell over? That doesn't make sense, Matthieu.'

'Probably not.' He turned away from her. 'I'm dealing with it.'

She put her hand on his shoulder and turned him to face her. Not knowing if doing something so intimate was the right way to go but doing it anyway. God, they'd kissed yesterday and now they couldn't speak to each other properly. 'Matthieu, please. Talk to me. What's going on?'

*Talk to me?* A phrase she'd had thrown at her enough in the past because she *never* talked about things. And yet here she was, pushing him for more.

He grimaced as if this conversation was costing him. 'I'm trying to stay calm, Rachel. You're in pain, you don't need me unloading on you as well.'

'I think I'd prefer it if you got it out of your system so we can move on. Tell me what the issue is. I hate tension.'

He looked away, then back at her, and shrugged wearily. 'The weather turned bad, but you didn't come back to base. You didn't use your locator beacon. You won't get a scan today. You don't want to stay with someone overnight for your own safety...'

She wasn't sure who was the most rattled. Him, because he clearly cared and didn't want to. Or her, because the emotion in his eyes connected deeply with something inside her. 'Hey, I told someone where I was going and what time to expect me back. I'm strong and fit and a damned good skier, as you know. If I'd really been in trouble, I'd have set off the locator beacon—'

'You weren't in trouble?' His voice rose and his eyes blazed. 'Out there, on your own, in a blizzard. Lost and in pain? What do you call a real emergency, Rachel? *Death?* Are you so independent that you're too proud to ask for help?' He shook his head. '*I'm* responsible for things that happen around here.'

'You're not responsible for me. No one is but me.' She glared back. But he cared enough to worry about her. That thought flooded her with warmth. 'I didn't think I needed rescuing. Please don't try to rescue me, Matthieu. I can look after myself.' That was it, she realised. He couldn't help but rescue people...after all those years with his mum when he hadn't been able to save her. Whether he realised it or not, he was still trying to save those he cared about.

He bristled, shoulders bunching. 'Why won't you let people help you?'

'I will absolutely admit if I'm in the wrong and am more than happy to accept responsibility for things I say and do. I was coming round to the fact that I was getting out of my depth and I, honestly, was about to set off the beacon just before you arrived.'

'But you didn't.' He threw his hands in the air.

'Because you arrived. Look, I'm independent, but I'm not stupid. I know what's within my capabilities and what isn't.' Then a thought struck her. She'd been so happy to be finally warm, and safe and looking forward to hot chocolate, that she'd said the first thing that had come into her head. Which was unusual for her, she was usually very careful about her word choices. But she'd said it. It was out there now. Even if she didn't feel it, it was a big, stupid, thing to say. 'Are you also angry because I said…um…that I love you?'

'Not at all.' His eyes widened and his throat worked. He looked totally blindsided. The playboy ensnared. He was a rescuer, but he didn't want to be shackled. 'It was obvious you were just grateful to us.'

'Exactly. I didn't mean…you know…that I *love* you, love you.'

'I know…' He breathed out, looking a lot brighter, a glimmer of a smile played on his lips. 'Cody's going to be heartbroken.'

'I somehow doubt that. And you promised me hot chocolate. Which, I might add—' she wanted so much to get back on a happier footing with him '—you still haven't produced.'

'Ah. Yes.' He relaxed just a little more. 'Medical treatment beats hot drinks every time. Give me ten minutes and you'll have one in your hand.' He helped her on to the back of the snowmobile, taking care to position her sore leg properly. 'You might want to hold on. Well, you might not want to, but you probably should.'

And there it was—neither of them knew where they stood or what the other person was really thinking and wanting. The accumulation of uncertainty, fear and total exhaustion was causing a major communication breakdown.

He climbed up in front of her and she snaked her arms round his waist, feeling the stretch and glide of his muscles as he steered down to the chalets. Remembering that the last time she'd had her arms around him, he'd been kissing her senseless.

Just how was she going to get back to that?

# CHAPTER ELEVEN

HIS LODGE WAS annexed at the side of the hotel complex. A huge three-bedroomed space with high wooden ceilings and whitewashed walls. Matthieu helped her along the corridor to a large open-plan lounge and sat her on a window seat in front of a window that looked out on to the resort and beyond. The clouds had cleared and the sun was setting, staining the sky with glorious soft peach and apricot hues.

She breathed in the view and smiled, trying to break the tension, digging deep inside her to make a first move to make things better between them. 'This weather is crazy. One minute you can't see anything, the next we have this.'

'It keeps us on our toes.' He turned to go, but she caught his fingers and he swivelled back to her, frowning. 'What is it, Rachel?'

*Here goes nothing.*

She squeezed his hand. 'Look, Matthieu. I'm sorry for today. Thank you for bringing me here and looking after me.'

'It's okay.' An eyebrow rose. 'It's my job.'

'It's above and beyond your job. So, again, thank you.'

'Not a problem.' But he hadn't let go of her hand and that gave her some hope.

Should she? Could she? She'd believed she could up there in the cold—it had been the only thing keeping her going. She couldn't stall now and let herself down. 'I was thinking, up on the mountain…'

His eyes narrowed. 'Sounds serious.'

'Actually, no. Not serious at all. I don't want to do anything serious ever again—not in my personal life anyway. I gave two years of my life to David only to learn that I'm not good at being part of a couple.' She took a breath. 'But I do want to have more fun and I think…what I hear about you and what I know about you…is that you like fun, too…'

'Louis been shooting his mouth off again?' His eyes glittered. But he was intrigued, she could see.

'It's common knowledge that you're…' She smiled. Knowing Matthieu wasn't wanting to commit to anyone made her feel a whole lot better about this. 'Let's just say, you're not ready to settle down yet.'

'No.' His eyes narrowed and he looked confused.

She could almost see his thought processes trying to join the dots. 'So, can we please forget today and rewind?'

'That depends.' His twinkling eyes narrowed. 'To when?'

'Back…on the sled. We were laughing then. And…' She held his gaze, feeling the most vulnerable and yet most alive she'd ever felt. 'Against the tree.'

His eyebrows shot up and his lips twitched. 'You want to kiss me again, Rachel?'

She was known for being forthright so here it was. Here *she* was. Asking for something she wanted. 'Yes. Yes, Matthieu, I'd like that very much.'

He sat on the edge of the banquette and took her hand, mock shock in his eyes. 'What? Even though you don't *love* me, love me?'

He smiled. No, grinned. A beautiful grin that lit up his whole face.

A mirroring smile glowed deep inside her and she almost forgot her pain. 'Even though I don't love you, Matthieu. I am more than happy to kiss you. Lots. If you want the same.'

'What about your space?'

'There was enough space on that mountain to last me a long time.' She flashed what she hoped was a rueful smile. 'Can we start over? I hate this tension between us.'

'Me, too.' He looked down and stroked her

hand for a moment, then looked back up at her. 'I'll go make that hot chocolate I promised you.'

Her heart clutched and she started to panic. He hadn't actually agreed to anything more. Had she just made a huge fool of herself? 'Are you escaping?'

He shook his head. 'Thinking.'

'You have to think about it?' Embarrassment spread through her. 'That is not a good sign.'

'Trust me, making you my famous hot chocolate is the biggest compliment you can get.' He leaned close and whispered, 'I don't need to think about it, Rachel. I was just planning where to start.'

Need rippled through her, pooling low and deep in her belly. 'And that is…?'

'You're still in pain and you've had quite an ordeal. Comfort first.' He brushed his fingers over her forehead, tucking some stray strands behind her ear, so gentle it made her heart squeeze and her stomach tighten with heat. Then he pressed his lips to her cheek.

'Wait.' She turned so her mouth was inches from his. 'Matthieu, I know exactly what's going to make me feel better.'

Then she reached her palm behind his head and drew him closer to take his mouth for one of those kisses they'd been talking about for too long.

She felt his smile against her lips and the deep

rumble of his laugh vibrating through her as he cupped her face and kissed her. Finally. Perfectly.

This kiss was gentle and exploring, his caress tender and caring, like a magic balm of heat and pleasure, stroking and stroking. She didn't know if it was the painkillers kicking in, or just the delicious pleasure of tasting Matthieu again, but all her aches seem to dissolve and she felt light and dizzy. Her skin prickled with shivers of excitement and her gut contracted with longing. She wound her arms round his neck, pressing her breasts against his chest, wanting his languid heat to reach every part of her.

Was this crazy? To want a man so much? To crave someone's touch? To dream about him? To let thoughts of him steer her off her path and down a mountain? Was she going crazy?

If so, she welcomed every wild thought running through her head right now: kissing, undressing, making love. Everything she'd been through today was worth this and every nerve ending tingled as she slid her hands over his shoulders, exploring hard muscles that held her in place, that she clung to.

But eventually he pulled away, tracing kisses along her collarbone like promises. 'It's been a hell of a day. You must be exhausted, Rachel.'

'I'll never be too tired for kissing.' She rested her head on his shoulder, her limbs liquid and her head a whirl of possibilities and wishes. She felt weirdly wired and yet sublimely relaxed. 'But I am…yes, actually shattered.'

'Not too tired for hot chocolate?' He kissed her again, lightly on the lips.

'After kissing, that's number two on my wish list right now.'

*'Mon plaisir.'* He dipped a kiss on her nose, then disappeared into the kitchen.

It was actually *her* pleasure. How was it that he could make her feel so breathy and light? So warm and yet excited with just a kiss?

How had she never felt like this kissing anyone else?

While he pottered in the kitchen, she took a moment to scan the room. She'd been expecting a typical man cave, all minimal monochrome, but this room was decorated in the same style as the rest of the hotel and chalets, in sumptuous warm shades and with luxurious fabrics. Mementoes from travels dotted shelves: exquisite hand-carved boxes and top-end Russian stacking dolls.

The walls held huge black and white photographs of cities—New York, Hong Kong, Singapore, Tokyo taken from arty angles—and had a signature at the bottom that she recognised as Matthieu's name. So, he was a man with an eye for the artistic as well as a businessman and all-round sporty outdoor guy.

'Is there no end to your talents?' she asked, pointing to the New York photo, as he brought through a tray with a silver jug that was like a tea-pot but taller, two steaming white porcelain mugs of delicious-smelling hot chocolate and a plate of bread and cheese. Her stomach growled, but his enigmatic smile made her hungry for something altogether different.

'The photos? I was just indulging my famous ego by blowing them up so big.' He handed her a mug and some food, then settled opposite her on the window seat, leaning back against the wall as he cut off a wedge of cheese and ate. 'You like them?'

'They're fabulous. Do you miss your old life?'

'Not at all. Although, I do miss the free travel. That was definitely a perk. Have you travelled much?'

'Oh… I guess so. I went away every school holiday. America, Thailand, Croatia, Greece… Lots.'

He tilted his head and smiled. 'Very lucky.'

'Kind of.' She silently mused over her difficult childhood and then remembered that she'd promised herself she'd be more open. She had to try to let him in and that meant letting something of herself out into the world. 'I suppose that sounds ungrateful, but after the divorce my parents played this sort of one-upmanship game—although neither admitted they did it.'

'What kind of game?'

'Who could take Rachel on the best holidays, hence the numerous ski vacations, too. Who could buy me the best presents. Basically, who was the best parent. But then they'd spend all holiday complaining about what the other parent had done or not done or said… In the end I used to beg to go to the kids' club each day just to get away from it all.' She laughed, although it wasn't funny. It never had been. She'd just wanted to stop being the thing they argued over, in front of, and about.

Matthieu's smile disappeared. 'For a few moments there I was jealous, but that sounds terrible.'

'It was. Not all kids' clubs are made equal. But I generally made some friends and hung out with children my own age, and if it was one of the awful clubs, I'd bury myself in a book. I did a lot of reading back then. The librarian at my local library said she'd never known anyone read so many books.' She dug deep for a smile. 'My parents did the same with birthday and Christmas presents, too: who spent the most, who bought the best present. Funny thing was, neither of them ever bought what I actually wanted.'

He sat forward, interested. 'Which was?'

'Ballet lessons. One of the series I loved reading the most was about a ballet boarding school. Oh, I dreamt about that place. Begged both parents to let me have lessons but, because I spent a week with Mum and a week with Dad, they couldn't agree on where I should go to dance school. Too close to Dad's and Mum would freak about how difficult it all was, too close to Mum's and Dad would complain about the traffic. It was just another thing for them to argue about. All well and good to be seen to give me the best, but another thing to actually give what I asked for. In the end I gave up asking. It was probably for the best. I mean, look at me.' She raised her braced knee. 'I'm a klutz. Do I look like I'd make a good ballerina?'

'Not unless it was a ballet about a hospital emergency department, *chérie*.' He laughed as he slid his hand over her leg as if it was the most natural thing in the world to do. It felt comfortable. Intimate. 'But it can't have been easy growing up in an environment like that. I can see why you'd withdraw into yourself if people were arguing around you.'

'They never stopped. They had a very volatile relationship...they loved hard and argued hard. I learnt to keep my own counsel from a very young age. I learnt how to entertain myself, to keep out of the way. I also learnt not to ask for anything, because I knew from experience that I wouldn't get it.'

'And you grew to depend only on yourself. I see that.'

'Apparently, it can be problematic.' She huffed out a breath, thinking suddenly of David, wishing she hadn't. But the more she thought about her failed relationship, the more she realised

David hadn't been the only villain in the piece. She'd never told him the things she'd just told Matthieu…silly hopes and dreams. Never really opened her heart to him. Matthieu made it easy to talk about things. He didn't judge. He empathised. He made her feel…safe.

'Oh, I don't know. You made your needs very clear just now.' Grinning, Matthieu leaned forward and put his lips to hers. 'You don't ever need to ask for kisses again. Just take them, Rachel. Whenever you want.'

She palmed his cheeks and stole another kiss. 'I'm going to hold you to that.'

'Good.' He gently lifted her sore leg and rested it on a cushion on his thigh. 'You need to keep it elevated.'

'Thank you, *Dr* LeFevre.' She laughed as he tickled her toes. Then she sipped the hot chocolate he'd laced with marshmallows and possibly some kind of liqueur. It was like no other hot chocolate she'd ever experienced. Along with the rich chocolatey taste there was a pop of something citrusy and something else…a deep, lush undertone that made her think of ice-cream, which was ridiculous because this was warm and lined her throat like velvet. She took another sip. Then another. 'This is incredible. I feel five hundred per cent better already.'

'I know. It makes everything better.'

'What's in it? I've got to make this at home.'

'I can't tell you.' He shook his head dramatically, grinning and tapping the side of his nose. 'Secret recipe.'

'There's something alcoholic in here, isn't there?'

'With you on painkillers? No way.' He frowned, but laughed, too. 'You're safe to drink it.'

'Secret recipe? Come on, Matthieu.' She nudged him with her foot. 'You have to tell me. I want to recreate this myself. It's like nectar from the gods. Heaven in a cup.'

'It's out of my hands.' He shrugged, palms upwards. 'Handed down from my mother and her mother before her. I'm sworn to secrecy.'

'It's divine. Really.' She drained her cup, hoping for a refill. Then realised he was looking over at a photograph in a silver frame on the coffee table. A young woman with a small boy on her knee. The boy was definitely Matthieu aged about four years old…an impish face and mischievous grin. The woman was looking directly into the camera and laughing. Carefree. She had the same large dark eyes as her son, the same-shaped mouth. 'She's beautiful. Your mother?'

'Yes.' He blinked and smiled softly. She liked that he loved his mum and felt a pang of envy. They'd clearly been close. She'd always wanted that kind of relationship with her parents and it still hurt that she couldn't have it.

'You miss her?'

'Of course.' But there was something else in his eyes.

'Matthieu…' With her heart in her throat, she touched his arm. 'You said she'd been sick. Was it cancer?'

He shook his head. 'She wasn't well her whole life, Rachel. One way or another. The kind of sickness that is unpredictable. Hard to have, hard to live with. She had bipolar disorder and depression. We had manic ups and very bad lows.'

*We.* He took it on board as his own issue to deal with too. 'Did she…?'

She didn't want to say the words in case she was jumping to conclusions or to hurt him too much by bringing up memories.

'Take her own life? Yes.' His eyes had darkened, his face hollowed out. He looked desperately sad and she found herself feeling the same. 'This time, I was too late.'

'You found her?' *This time.* Which meant there'd been other times, too. Her hand went to her chest—how utterly unbearable.

'Yes. I'd only left her for a few hours to come up here and sort some things out. She'd waved me off and told me she was fine. She hadn't been great, you know? But I'd left her before, many times…' His throat worked and he looked desolate. 'She'd taken pills, a bottle of cognac. There was nothing I could do.'

'God, Matthieu, that's awful. No wonder you're

so protective.' This explained why he felt responsible for everyone, needed to keep them safe…
even though he tried to keep away, he couldn't
help himself. She was beginning to understand.

He rubbed his jaw. 'I should have stopped her.
I should have known.'

'You can't believe that any of it was your fault.'

'I should have known things weren't going
well. I learnt early on to read her micro expressions.' He shook his head. 'So I could tell what
mood she was in. What kind of a day it was going
to be. Whether she needed help or not. She'd be
fine for a while—months at a time—take her
tablets and everything would be happy. But then
she'd stop taking the meds because she felt okay
and said she didn't need them. Trust me, she was
not okay.'

'I can't imagine how that was for you.'

'As a five-year-old you want routine. As an
eight-year-old you want her to get help. As a teenager you don't want anyone to see or know about
it—cruel, I know, but it was how I felt. Christmases were unpredictable. One year I'd be over-
whelmed by expensive gifts she couldn't afford.
Another year she'd be so debilitated we wouldn't
have presents or even food.'

He hauled in a breath.

'But we got by. I helped… I hope I helped. As I
moved into my early twenties she was doing well.
She had a boyfriend, he was kind and he helped

her with her meds. Things were straightened out for a year. Two. Three. When I got the job offer in Paris I turned it down at first, but she heard about it from Louis's parents and insisted I take it. A job of a lifetime, she'd said.'

'She was right.'

'Yes. I had friends here who kept an eye on her and, of course, I spoke to her every day and came back most weekends and holidays. But she'd get angry with me for coming home all the time. Told me I didn't trust her. And she'd been okay, you know? Taking her tablets regularly, looking after herself. So, I started to travel a bit more. Relax.'

He looked down at his hands. 'Then the relationship with Gilbert ended and she started to decline. She stopped talking to me, refused to see anyone, so I came home. She was in a bad state, but I managed to get her some medical help and she was okay. For the year I was with her she was okay. Then one day she wasn't.' He paused, grief sliding into every hollow in his face. 'I hadn't seen the signs, I didn't know.'

'Sometimes there aren't any signs, Matthieu.'

'I should have known.' Guilt bit at his features. 'I was always alert around her. I found her twice already, hell… I should have seen it coming.'

'It wasn't your fault. You have to know that.'

He shrugged as if he heard her, but didn't agree. 'Now I'm on my own. I have no one to be responsible for, no one to worry about. And thank God for that.'

'And that's why you couldn't commit to a relationship, isn't it? Because you had to always think about your mum, about coming home.'

'No… It's because I didn't have space for anyone else. I didn't want…*don't* want to carry that responsibility for someone else ever again.' He stared out of the window for a few beats, then turned to her with a wry smile. 'Good job we're just about the fun, right?'

She laughed and stroked his arm. 'Maybe… the better you get to know someone, the more fun you can have.'

She couldn't believe she was saying this…feeling this. Because she'd been trying hard not to let anyone know her at all. But with Matthieu that was getting harder and harder every moment she spent with him. There was something about him that made it impossible not to talk, to share, to open up. His gentle questions, his interest and genuine concern. And she felt the more they shared the better it would get.

Wow. Maybe this was Rachel Tait finally learning how to get close to someone. Talking. Sharing. Being honest and admitting how she felt about things instead of bottling them up. It was liberating and wonderful and yet wildly exposing.

But safe. Always safe, even in her most vulnerable moments. She knew Matthieu treasured her…it was evident in the way he looked at her, his touch. That he accepted her, faults and all.

'I'm sure we can have lots of fun getting to know each other. Especially physically…' Matthieu laughed as he kissed her again, but then grimaced. 'I'm sorry. You didn't need to hear all that. It's not something I generally speak about… although, of course, it's no secret. Everyone in the village knew her and knew our story. They collectively kept an eye on me growing up…so Louis tells me. Because she couldn't always do that. Sometimes, like the difficult Christmases, they'd drop off food and small gifts. When I think back, there were other gestures, too—tickets to a football game, toys they were "throwing out" and did I want them?'

'They love you, that's obvious.'

He blinked. 'I owe them a lot.'

'Hence the resort and the jobs for locals.'

'That's part of my motivation, yes. Funny thing is, I tried to hide it all. Thought I'd covered it all up, but her problems were well known. Nothing's private here. Not even pain.'

'It's a pain shared, though. That's got to help, even just a little bit, to know that someone else— a whole village—cares about you?' Even though he'd had a deeply personal loss he'd had a community round him. God, if only she'd had that and had someone else help carry her load.

But then, looking back, she'd collapsed in on

herself and not reached out. Maybe she should take a leaf out of Matthieu's book and try to do that more?

And risk rejection? Like David? Like her father? Her mother?

And yet, find the right people, dare to share and you have a home. A place where you belong.

Where did she belong?

Nowhere.

Matthieu stroked her hand. 'That's enough about me.'

'Thank you for telling me.' It was all so sad and yet the simple act of talking and listening had brought them closer. They'd both suffered trauma, but had dealt with it differently. She was amazed at his strength and his capacity to give so much. There was no doubt he had adored his mother.

There was also no doubt as to why he didn't commit to anyone else. He needed to be free from having to think about someone else. Who could blame him?

He was a good man. Quite possibly the nicest man she'd ever met. He genuinely cared about people, about making them comfortable and relaxed. He was kind...he'd taken her on the sled just to make her smile. He took time to help people. And yet he'd been through so much sadness it made her heart hurt for him.

For a few moments they sat in peaceful silence,

hugging their mugs to their chests and admiring the view. She didn't feel a need to fill the space.

Eventually, he turned to her and stroked his fingers on her cheek. 'Hey. You look beat. Early night?'

He clearly wasn't about to make a move and that was okay. She didn't think it was the right time for anything even more intense, so she decided to leave him with his memories and thoughts. She hefted her sore leg to the floor and stood up, gripping the banquette cushion for balance. 'Yes, but first I'm going for a bath. Wish me luck.'

'Hey...' He caught her hand. 'You okay?'

She cupped his face. 'I'm fine, Matthieu.'

'Fine?' His eyes narrowed in a warning and she laughed, knowing exactly what he meant.

'By which I mean, thank you, you've been amazing. My stomach is full, my heart is full. But my leg and back are painful. I think a long soak would be a very good thing.'

'Of course. Take this with you.' He poured more chocolate from the silver jug into her mug and gave it to her. 'If you need any more, just shout.'

She hugged the cup close to her chest. 'A girl could get used to this kind of treatment.'

'Hey, please don't go throwing yourself at trees just to get the chance for hot chocolate in the bath. Just ask next time, okay?' Then he stood and wrapped her in his arms and held her. Just held her there and she held on, too.

A girl could get used *to this*, she thought.

But it probably wasn't the best idea she'd had.

# CHAPTER TWELVE

WELL, HE'D PROBABLY blown it.

They were supposed to be having fun and no doubt he'd scared her off with his tales.

But, despite what she thought, she wasn't closed off, she was quiet, thoughtful. Reluctant to share, but when she did, she had so much to contribute.

And was sexy as hell. And wanted no strings.

She was perfect.

He cleared up the tray, finished getting the guest room ready, then flicked through his music app for something she might like… He smiled, probably not the time for bellowing God-awful songs from the eighties—

*'Aaargh!'*

A crash. In the bathroom. Something breaking. A splash.

His heartrate tripled as he ran to the closed bathroom door. What was he going to find? Images flashed through his head…images he wanted to forget but were branded on to his brain. 'Rachel! Rachel! Are you okay?'

'Don't come in!' She sounded anxious, but also as though she was laughing, too.

Was she hysterical? 'Rachel! What's happened?'

'Just don't. I'm…it's okay. I'm just—ow!' She cursed. There was more squeaking and splashing and more groans and he couldn't bear to wait any longer. He pushed the door open a crack. 'Can I—?'

A pause. Then… 'Okay. But don't look.'

He shoved the door wide and stopped, trying not to look, but catching a glimpse. Adrenalin slowing, then ramping. 'What the hell? Rachel?'

'Don't look!' She was immersed in the water, completely covered by bubbles, her hair plastered to her head in wet tendrils, bubbles caught on her head and shoulders, on her eyelids and chin. The spa jets were firing at full speed, creating even more bubbles that were scooting over the edge of the tub and on to the floor. 'I slipped getting in, trying to protect my knee. And got a total dunking under the water and knocked the mug on to the floor with my good foot. I'm so sorry, Matthieu. I hope it wasn't a good one.'

'It wasn't.' He looked to where she was pointing, to a puddle of hot chocolate and broken porcelain, and raised his hand. 'Don't get out. You'll cut yourself.'

'Honestly, don't worry.' She bit her lip and then grimaced. 'I was going to clear it up when I got out. I was hoping you hadn't heard me, and I could get away with hiding the pieces underneath in the rubbish bin.'

'Hiding the evidence? I'd have caught you eventually.' She was smiling ruefully and he shook his head in mock frustration. 'And doing it with a bad foot? Hopping on a wet floor would be even more dangerous.'

He dashed to the kitchen for a dustpan and kitchen roll and started to clear the mess up, all the while acutely aware of her sinking under the water, washing her hair, sluicing the shampoo off. Doing something else splashy, which he assumed was washing.

Far more aware of her than he should have been.

She was naked. Wet. Covered in bubbles. She wanted to kiss him.

His whole body burned for her.

He couldn't remember a time when he'd wanted someone this much. Not kissing her before had almost killed him, but he'd wanted to give her time. Give himself time to think about her offer.

God, since when did he have to think about kissing someone who was offering it?

But this was Rachel, and he was drawn to her in a way he'd never been drawn to a woman before. He didn't know what to do with the feelings in his chest every time he looked at her. She'd had a rough life with her parents and her douchebag ex. She needed more than he could give. And she wanted to give so much too, he could see.

He saw it in her eyes. Saw everything in her

eyes. The vulnerability she tried to hide. The pain of her past. The simmering need that turned her irises from soft grey to shimmering silver. And he felt an answering need deep inside himself. A burning, burnished golden desire, bright and hot, that flickered into life whenever she was around and a good amount of time when she wasn't as his thoughts strayed to her, over and over.

She was naked. Two feet away from him.

This was pure torture.

After a few minutes he heard, 'Matthieu—can you pass me a towel for my hair?'

'Sure.' Trying to stay calm, he grabbed a hand towel and, without looking at her, shoved it behind him.

'Um…' She laughed. 'Matthieu… I'm over here.'

'Where?' He turned to find her reclining at the opposite end of the bath and was paralysed by the sight of her bare skin, the regal neck, the smooth décolletage and soft swell of her breasts peeking out above the water. No more bubbles.

He handed her the towel and turned away. No way should he be looking at her like that. 'Right, I'm going. Call if you need more help.'

'Will do. Oh? Oh, God.'

'What is it?' He found himself turning back to her.

Her mouth formed a horrified 'O' as she covered her breasts with an arm before sliding further under the water. 'I thought…where have all the bubbles gone?'

'That happens…with shampoo and soap…it's the cationic and anionic charges…positive and negative…makes the bubbles collapse…' He'd looked away again, but couldn't shake the memory of that creamy skin, the dark nipples. Hot arrows of need shot through him. *God.* She was divine.

Not touching her was killing him.

'Ouch. This bath is so not comfortable with a bad back.' She sat up sharply and lent forward, her back to him.

And he was just about to leave, he really was, but his eyes fixed on her spine at her groan. His gut lurched at the sight. '*Dieu,* Rachel. Your back is a map of bruises.'

'Is it? It's pretty sore. Where? Can you check, please? Is it bad?' She reached her arm round to her back. 'Lower rib?' Can you point to where it's worse? See if that's where the pain's coming from.'

He swallowed back his desire—the woman needed his help—and gently grazed her bruised skin with his fingertip, trying not to hurt her. 'Here?'

She flinched. 'Ouch. Yes.'

He thought about pressing his lips to that very spot, or any part of her—*all* of her—but clamped down on those thoughts, too. '*Je suis désolé.*'

'Don't be sorry. It wasn't your fault. Is it really bad? Where?'

'It's very bruised. I think I can see Italy there and...um... Australia.' At her bidding he ran his fingers down the pearls of her spine, chasing drips of water, tracing down to the small of her back and then up again, dipping carefully over black and blue smudges. 'Russia's kind of warped and I think Spain's melted into Morocco.'

'That can't be good.' She shivered, and her skin erupted in goosebumps, but she didn't move away. 'Whatever river your fingers are tracing is making me ticklish.'

'Rachel—' He swallowed again. This was probably completely inappropriate. But he was human and she was gorgeous. *But broken.* In too many ways. With some sense seeping back into his brain, he edged back from her. 'Sorry. Look, the guest room's down the hall on the left. I'll see you in the morning.'

'Matthieu...wait.' Her hand slid over his, catching his fingers the way she had earlier, a grip that was firm and yet soft. Warm skin, a flutter of fingertips, that had him imagining those hands on the rest of his body.

'Yes?' He met her eyes to study her expression. Was she going to ask him to join her? Tell him to get the hell out?

She pulled a face. 'I think I'm going to need help to get out. It's just... I can't take weight on my bad foot and I should probably have had a shower, but I do love bubbles and the spa jets are amazing.'

'Call me when you need me.'

The spa jets whirred off. 'Matthieu.' Her voice was cracked and sex-laden. There was a moment when it felt as if the atmosphere hung around them, imbued with frank desire.

'Yes?' His voice sounded rough and thick in the muggy, too-bright bathroom.

Her eyes snagged his and she looked at him, so flagrantly in need of kissing that it almost took his breath away. 'I need you.'

With those three words something inside him burst into flames. The air crackled around them so thick he could almost touch it.

'Sure thing.' Reining in his desire—at least, trying to—he grabbed a towel and held it up for her to step into, but of course, climbing out of a bath with one working foot was a lot harder than climbing in. She cursed and wobbled and gripped his arm and eventually, she was out, wrapped in a towel and squeaky clean.

She looked so beautiful, her cheeks all pink with the heat, her eyes glittering with water drops, and she must have seen whatever was in his eyes because she sighed on a secretive smile. 'About that map. If Russia was here...' she took his hand and guided it behind her to her ribs '...following a line of latitude...then Canada must be...' she slid his hand across her ribs to the curve of her breast '...about here?'

'I don't need a damned geography lesson,' he growled into her damp hair, struggling to control his overactive libido. Then, unable to stop himself, he pressed her against the wall and palmed her damp breast. 'I know exactly where I want to be.'

With a strangled moan Rachel lifted her mouth to his and kissed him, hard. She couldn't wait any longer. Wouldn't wait. *Take it*, he'd said. Now she was going to hold him to his word.

He tasted of the sultry hot chocolate and his own Matthieu tang of spice and heat. So intoxicating she wanted to drown in him. His fingertips down her spine, the way he looked at her, made her hungry for him. Desperate.

His tongue slid into her mouth, taking the kiss deeper and more frantic, and before she could stop or think she was peeling his sweater and T-shirt off in a rush of need and urgency.

She ran her hands over his back, down his chest, feeling the way his muscles moved as he pressed her against the wall. The toned biceps that held her there. The strong thigh muscles pressing against her legs. The hard swell against her thigh. Taking his mouth again, she wriggled closer so she could feel him press at her core.

She wanted his mouth on her, everywhere. His

hands touching her everywhere. She wanted him deep inside her.

This need for him, shocking and bright and raw, made no sense and yet it made perfect sense. It was everything. He was everything.

But there was so much about him she still didn't know, so much she *did* know that she was attracted to. So much he'd endured, taken on as his burden just to help ease his mother's suffering. Then built the resort as a gift of gratitude to those who had helped him.

And as he'd trusted her with his story she'd wanted to cry with him, to ease his pain...wanted to stop him from walking into that room where his mother was, a full body block so she could have taken those shockwaves of grief for him. She'd burned with sadness and yet saw, *felt* the hidden light inside him that drove him to fight for those he loved.

And she'd wanted that light to burn for her, too. She still did.

Her towel slipped...or had she let it slip? She didn't know. But here she was, naked, in front of him. Enjoying, relishing, the way he looked at her with raw need and promise in his gaze.

Doing this was crazy...inviting rejection. She didn't open herself up like this, she closed herself off. Kept herself safe. But something about the way he was looking at her spurred her on.

Made her feel special, sexy. Wanted. Safe. *That* was intoxicating.

He bent down and slid his hands under her knees and whipped her into his arms. She laughed. 'Whoa, caveman. I can walk.'

A deep rumble of laughter burst from his throat as he kicked her discarded brace out of the way. 'Actually, *chérie*, you can't.'

Then he strode…fast…into his bedroom.

She'd imagined this moment countless times over the last few days, imagined the way his bedroom would be, the way he'd look at her, the way she'd feel, but none of her imaginings had come close to the reality.

His room was lit by two nightlights that cast a dreamy sheen over the room. Her eyes fixed on his, her mouth on his, she didn't spare any glances at the decor. Didn't care. His sheets were cool and soft. The mattress giving just enough as he laid her down as if she were something precious.

Sliding his hands out from under her, he lay down next to her, his top half gloriously naked, smooth skin defining hard abs.

The look on his face as he traced his fingers between her breasts undid her completely. That was something she hadn't anticipated. Such hunger. Raw emotion. As if he was close to the edge and didn't know whether to cling on tight or let go and let himself fall. As if she was the only person in the world who would catch him.

Biting her lip, her breath coming in short gasps, she ran fingertips down his belly, over his jeans zipper where she cupped his erection. The light in his eyes ignited. He caught her fingers in his hand the way she did to him. 'Wait, Rachel...'

'No. Can't wait.' She tugged at him, pulled him down over her so she could feel the beautiful weight, the press, the heat, the length of him. 'Waited too long. The water almost went cold while you cleared up the mess. And I waited and waited for you.'

He grinned, sexy as hell. 'I didn't know if you wanted me to join you, or just act as your chambermaid.'

'I wanted you to join me about three hours ago. Yesterday. Last week.' She kissed his jaw, his cheek, his mouth, knowing she'd never have enough of his taste.

He laughed. 'We've got all night, *chérie.*'

'Then let's make every minute count, *chéri*.' She parroted his word, feeling his laughter rumble through her, and she couldn't help but laugh, too. This was insane and yet so completely right.

She stroked his erection again, slipping her hand into the space between denim and skin, felt the twitch of his body away and also toward her fingers, felt the shudder of his groan against her cheek. And his hand gripping hers, taking it from his jeans. 'No. Rachel. Wait.'

*Ray Shell.*

'If you could just say my name again and again that would make me happy for ever. I don't think I need anything else.'

'We'll see about that.' He grinned, then nuzzled against her throat. 'Rachel. *Rachel.*'

'*God,* Matthieu.' She giggled. Undone, unwrapped and unravelled. 'Yes. Anything. Yes. *Yes.*'

He kissed down to her breasts, sucking in first one nipple, then the second, making her arch against him, the sensation of teeth and wet against her tender skin making her dizzy with desire. Then his mouth went lower, a dazzling tease of nips and kisses to her belly, lower…to her thigh, her inner thigh.

He pushed her legs apart and kissed between her legs, sending jolts of heat spiralling through her. His tongue and his fingers explored her, slipping inside her, and all she knew was this moment, the sensuous pleasure of his hands, his mouth.

And then he slowed the pace, teasing her, making her think about begging. Rachel Tait didn't beg. Rachel Tait didn't ask for anything, she took it. She didn't call out. She didn't show her emotions. She didn't do needy. She didn't do desperate. She kept everything inside, in a tight knot. But Matthieu made her feel everything, want everything.

But he waited. Then he teased some more and

she squirmed against his hand. Then he waited again, hot breath on her thigh, pleasure–pain rasp of his stubble on her skin, the pressure of his fingers against her most sensitive parts.

'Matthieu.' She half laughed, half sobbed his name, desperate now.

'What do you want? Say it.'

Her fingers tightened in his hair. 'Don't stop.'

But he'd already stopped and she was going out of her mind with need. Then he teased again. 'Tell me what you want, Rachel.'

Rachel Tait didn't beg.

Not until she screamed, '*Please*. Matthieu. *Please*. More.'

'*Mon plaisir*, Rachel.'

Nothing had ever felt this good. She felt him murmur her name against her skin once, twice, as he slid his fingers deep into her and then she was slipping, rising, flying, moaning, gripping his hair as he brought her to the edge, then took her over. And over. And over. Shattering her into pieces only he would be able to fit together again.

For a few moments she lay there, trying to breathe, to force air into a body that shook. She suddenly felt weirdly emotional and blinked back tears that had sprung from nowhere. 'What are you doing to me, Matthieu?' she asked him, again half laughing, half sobbing. All his.

'Hopefully something good?' He kissed his way back up her body, but when he saw her face his smile dropped. He kissed a rogue tear slipping down her cheek. 'What's happened? What's wrong?'

'Nothing at all. Everything is perfect.' It was. Like nothing she'd ever imagined. This feeling in her heart, through her body, dizzy with release and also more greedy need. She breathed against his chest, inhaling his scent that drove her crazy, then she looked up at him and traced the lips that had given her so much pleasure. 'Stupid tears. I don't know why this is happening.'

'What are you feeling? Tell me.' He stroked her face so tenderly it made more tears spring.

What was happening? How did something so amazing make her want to cry?

Speaking her truth about deep, personal things was new territory. She never did that, preferring to keep deeply private things close to her chest.

But she found her voice through a thick, full throat, not sure if she even knew the words to describe this emotion. Or had the wherewithal to say those words out loud. But she tried, because he asked. And she trusted him not to reject her. She trusted him.

Wow. That was a first for the Ice Queen. 'I feel…like…something new. Someone new. Someone…free, like a bird. Or freer, at least. I'm not making sense. You can't ask me questions like that after you've done such amazing things to me. I'm having trouble saying anything at all.'

He laughed. 'My free bird. I think I understand.' Then he took her hand and placed it over his heart. 'Fly high, *chérie*. Enjoy the ride.'

*'Oui. Bien sur.'* Of course, she'd enjoy the ride if he was her travelling companion. 'And…*merci*, Matthieu. *Merci pour tout.*' For everything he'd done, he'd said, for the way he made her feel.

'Good effort.' He blinked, smiling at her French. 'As I've said many times, it's my pleasure…to give you pleasure.'

Then he cupped her face and kissed her. His tongue dancing with hers in sultry circles that hypnotised her, stoked the heat inside her, until she couldn't think straight, didn't know her own name.

The kiss changed, slowed, softened into a caress she felt in every part of her. A prayer. Worship. Tender. Her body trapped by his arms, her heart captured by his soul.

Breathless, he pulled away, eyes smudged with desire. 'And your leg? Your back?'

'Shoot!' She clamped her hand over her mouth. 'I'd forgotten about them. Or at least, the pain doesn't seem so bad when you're having an orgasm.'

'Or the drugs are working.' Grinning, he stroked her nipple, then he bent and sucked it in, making her squirm in delight. 'We haven't even started yet.'

'That is very good news. Because I want you,

Matthieu.' She pulled him to face her again. 'And I want you to feel the way I just did.'

'Pretty sure I already do. I almost lost it just watching you come.'

'I want to watch you come, too.' She laughed, surprised to be talking like this. David never talked like this. They only ever had sex in the dark, in a sort of hushed reverence. She'd thought that was all she needed. Believed it was enough. How wrong she'd been.

She snapped her eyes closed for a second and refused to allow any more thoughts of him into her head. Then she tiptoed her fingertips down Matthieu's stomach. 'But I think it'll only work if I wasn't the only one naked.'

'Ah. Yes.' He looked down at his jeans and his hand went to his zip, but she stopped him. 'Let me.'

'Be my guest.' Laughing, he lay back, arms behind his head, a very smug expression on his face, and she loved that he was playful and fun and yet could be serious and deep. She sat up and tugged at his zip, inching it slowly down, watching him watching her. In control, but hanging on by a thread. Knowing she turned him on made her feel the sexiest she'd ever felt.

She helped him wriggle out of his jeans and then his boxers, and he was so hard and yet silky soft to her touch. She took him in her hands and stroked. Slowly. He groaned, his laughter dying and his eyes misting. His back arched at each stroke. '*Mon Dieu*, Rachel. You make me want so much. I want to be inside you. Deep inside.'

'Yes.' Nothing else mattered now. She would ask, she would tell, she would take. She would beg for more of this, more of him. '*Please*, Matthieu.'

'*Attends*. Wait.' He touched her hand. 'You'll have to let go. Condom,' he clarified.

'Gotcha.' It was too long since she'd done this. Laughing, she shifted sideways while he rolled to the edge of the bed, magicked a condom from somewhere and sheathed.

Within seconds he was back, tucking her underneath him, his gaze a burnished gold of intent and desire. He lowered his head and sealed his mouth over hers in a kiss that was carnal and feral and possessive. His erection nudged at her centre and she writhed her hips against his in anticipation and encouragement.

But he paused, running his palms over her forehead, smoothing her hair. 'Rachel, are you sure about this?'

'Never been more sure about anything. Please, Matthieu.' She angled her hips and then, yes! He was pushing into her, filling her, stroke after slow, sensuous stroke. Sensations rippled through her: his mouth on hers, his stubble on her jaw, the long thick glide of him inside her, the heat. His taste.

She'd been wrong before; nothing had ever felt *this* good.

Something flickered in his eyes as he held her gaze, something he didn't say, but she felt deep inside her soul. Something pure and new. Then he groaned into her hair, 'Rachel… Rachel…' and his rhythm kicked up. She met him beat for beat, thrust for thrust, angling her hips so he could go deeper.

'Matthieu…' She clung to him, fingers digging deep into his shoulders, pinning him there, part of her. And he clung to her, his hands clasping her arms.

'Rachel…' He drove into her harder and faster and she felt herself losing her grip on control, spiralling higher and higher. Then he called her name one more time before she felt his final thrust, a ripple deep, deep inside her as he found his release.

For a few moments he held her close as he hauled in breath after breath. Then he finally relaxed and slid sideways, his arms never letting go of her.

She lay still, not wanting to move, never wanting to leave this bed again. Completely spent, she breathed out and smiled, feeling sleepy and relaxed and utterly, thoroughly sated. 'That was amazing. I don't think I've ever felt like this before.'

'Then you've been doing it wrong.' He winked, but something about the mist in his eyes made her think none of this was a joke to him. 'Next time, I want to undress you. That's part of the fun.'

*Next time.* 'Do you want me to get dressed now, so you can strip me later?'

'No.' He hauled her tighter against him. 'Do not get dressed again. Ever.'

'I'm going to get pretty cold up that mountain, naked.'

'Hush.' He put his finger to her mouth. 'Don't talk about work. Or about anything out there. Out there does not exist. What do you need, here, right now?'

*I need kissing. I need someone to talk to and to listen. Someone to care. I don't want to be on my own any more. I need this.*

She realised then that she needed understanding and connection. And she got it from Matthieu.

*I need you.*

Tears filled her eyes. She'd never felt as if she'd needed anyone before. Not like this. Not this gnawing ache of anticipation and joy. It meant something, she knew. And yet she didn't want to know, didn't want to push it into more than it could be.

She kissed him languidly, pressing herself against him. 'I need more sex, please.' But then stifled a yawn as fatigue bled into her bones. 'Oops…sorry. I think I might need a little nap first.'

'Then sleep, Rachel.' He ran his hand down her

spine and kissed her throat, her neck, her shoulder. 'You need rest, *chérie*. You've had a big day.'

Not just a big day. A big revelation. She'd been trying to hide from him, trying to keep herself safe and intact, closed off and aloof. But he'd broken her open with a kiss, shattered her with sex and seen through to her core. No...worse, *more*, she'd taken him by the hand and willingly shown him, told him. Begged and demanded. And she didn't care.

There were no regrets, not for this.

# CHAPTER THIRTEEN

'MATTHIEU…'

He wasn't sure if he was dreaming or if this was real, but Rachel Tait was in his bed and her hand was stroking down his bare thigh.

*Reality check.*

It wasn't a dream. She was still here, tucked into the crook of his arm. He fitted himself against her soft curves, warm skin. '*Chérie*…you okay? Any pain?'

'A little. My knee's throbbing, but I'm okay. Are you?'

'Yes,' he groaned into hair that smelt of the resort verbena shampoo and tickled his nose. It was the best he'd felt in his whole life. She hadn't moved into the spare room as he'd thought she might, she'd settled against him and fallen asleep. First time he was glad a woman had stayed over. First time he'd wanted one to. It was now three forty-five, they were enveloped in a soupy darkness. There was no noise, no light. It felt as if the whole world was comprised of just the two of them. 'Never felt better.'

'Good.' A pause. Then she laughed. 'Everything feels different here.'

'In what way?'

'It's like my senses are on full alert. The sun is brighter. The snow is whiter. The sky is so beautiful and it is very, very dark in this room. So dark I can almost grasp it.'

'You want me to put a light on?'

'No. It's just disorientating.' Her bottom snuggled against his groin. 'Or maybe it's this situation that's got me a bit off balance.'

'Me, too.' But to make sure she knew it was a good off balance he squeezed her tight and kissed her neck. 'We've applied to get dark sky reserve recognition. Come look outside.'

After activating a wall light with his phone app, he handed her a robe, then opened the heavy curtains. Rachel slipped the robe over her shoulders and he helped her hop across the carpet to the window where she leaned against him, craning her neck to peer out at the creamy purple trail of the Milky Way. 'Wow. It's amazing.'

'Wait.' He turned off the light with the app and then held her close. 'Look at all those stars, all those planets out there. Pretty special, eh? Stretched across the globe…the Earth's roof holding us all safe. If ever I'm travelling and I see this, I feel right at home.'

She sighed. 'To be honest, I've never really felt like I've had a proper home. I might give this a go when I'm back in my apartment. It might make me feel as if I do belong somewhere. Unfortunately, we don't have dark skies like this where I live in Leeds, there's too much light pollution.'

But he was stuck on her previous words. 'No home? Mine was difficult…tragic even, but it was still my home. I can't imagine how it feels to not have a special place.'

'I'm working on it. I have plans. I'm going to sell the flat I shared with David, then I'll buy something just for me. Finally. Growing up, I had two homes. Just two houses really, because neither of them felt like a place where I could properly relax. Although, things got a little better when Mum and Dad eventually split up.'

'The arguing was hard to live with?'

She nodded. 'The silences, too. I hated them, because they meant my parents were simmering and it would only be a matter of time before the explosion. And there was always an explosion, Matthieu.' She shuddered. 'Silence is scary.'

'I understand. It was all or nothing with my mum, too. Silences were the worst because I never knew what she was doing…' He switched off the flashing images running through his head. 'Or had…done.' Three times she'd tried to take her own life over the years and he'd found her each time.

That was the reason he didn't believe in all that love stuff. Love hadn't been enough to stop his mother killing herself. It hadn't been enough to keep her in this world, in *his* world. For him. Love hadn't stopped his heart shattering. It had just made everything worse.

'I can't imagine, Matthieu. I just can't. But I want you to know that I'm so sorry.' She stroked his cheek. 'I wish there was something I could do to help.'

'It's done, Rachel. I just live with it. I try to re-member the best times.' Because remembering that day, reliving it over and over, would bring him to his knees.

'I'm so glad you had some good times.' She smoothed his hair and smiled. 'I want you to have so many more. I want you to have the very best full life. That way you live for her, too.'

She understood. Sure, she didn't know what it felt like to lose a parent, but she knew what it was like to live with that fear that the world was going to implode at any moment. She wanted to help. Just knowing that was like liquid heat in his chest. He cupped her face and kissed her, soft and slow. 'Thank you.'

They stood together in the dark, staring up at the endless sky, and he felt it might be the right time to ask her, 'You really aren't close to either of your parents? Tell me some more, please. I want to know *you*.'

He made sure to put the emphasis on you and she blinked up at him. 'Are you sure?'

'Of course. I've made love to you, shared my bed with you, I want to know who the real Rachel Tait is and that means knowing more about your past.'

Her smile told him she was being brave, but she clearly didn't want to go there. 'It's not something I talk about. I never even told David. People don't understand.'

'Try me. I've told you everything about me and my *maman*.' There wasn't much to tell. He'd tried to save her and he'd failed.

'Okay...' She gave him a wobbly smile. 'The thing you have to understand is that they met and married within a few weeks. One of those passionate all-consuming loves, but it quickly withered and then their hate was all consuming, too. Powerful, destructive. There were affairs, reconciliations. Crockery thrown against the wall. Rage. Then one day I begged them to just stop, told them I couldn't take it any more and I made my dad leave. He got remarried first. In some ways it was a relief to have him focus on someone else, although it didn't stop the arguing. At that point it felt like he'd given up on the one-up-manship thing and now I was just a problem he didn't want to be around.'

'Never.' Matthieu's grip on her tightened. He ached to show her just how much she mattered.

'Mum met and married Ken when I was sixteen. She was so besotted with him I sort of faded from her life. Until my wedding, of course. They both insisted on coming to that, even though I knew it was going to be a war zone. I made them promise not to speak to each other. I was so nervous about the whole thing. Mainly…if I'm honest, about making them proud of me. Being happy for *me*. Seeing me for who I am. Not a problem to be argued over. It felt, when Dad walked me up the aisle, that I'd finally got that father–daughter thing going… You know, the one where there's an inseparable bond, where he'll fight anyone on your behalf? The one where you're always his little girl and he means it, truly means it, instead of using it as ammunition to get his own way. Well, of course you don't know because you're not a woman.'

'I get the drift.' He'd wanted that parent–child bond, too. Had it for a while with his mum, but she'd become so ill he'd ended up looking after her.

Rachel's shoulders bunched forward. 'Then David did his disappearing act and I was left looking like an idiot.'

'What did they say? Please tell me they were supportive.'

'Dad was furious and said he'd been humiliated in front of everyone…as if it was all about him and not my life that had been ruined. He certainly did fight for me. He roared, making everything worse, but he took it as a sign to leave early and get back to his wife…who'd refused to come to the wedding because my mum was going to be there. I don't think I'll see him again for a long time.' She breathed in and then exhaled deeply, as if trying to stay in control, but her shaking hands gave her away. 'Mum was a little more support- ive. In as much as, after the initial shock and three stiff whiskies, she said it was a shame, but I was lucky to escape someone who didn't love me.'

'She was right about that.' It astounded him that anyone could not see Rachel. That she had to wish for affection.

'True. Then she added that I would be bet- ter on my own because that's what I've always been. That she'd marvelled at how much time I could spend in my room, just reading and ignor- ing the world.' She bit her bottom lip at the mem- ory. 'Like she wasn't the reason for it in the first place. And that perhaps I should be more giving in my relationships and then people would like me more. Then she left. She didn't hug me or help me, she just looked at me as if she'd expected it all along—that I was my father's daughter.'

A vice tightened around Matthieu's chest. She looked so sad he wanted to do something, any- thing, to erase that pain. To rail at her parents for making her feel this way. He tipped her chin to look into her eyes. 'How did you react? Please tell me you did your famous Dr Blowout?'

'There was no point. They don't want to hear

what I have to say. I did what I always do and
pushed the disappointment down inside me. Gave
her a kiss and waved her off, promising her I was
okay. Because it looked like that was what she
needed to hear. I saved my anger for my texts to
David.'

'I can't even compute this.'

'It's what happens.' Her shrug and acceptance
made his heart twist.

'No, it isn't.'

'It's what happens to me. I'm used to it. I deal
with it. That whole wedding disaster just proved
that I can't rely on anyone. I'm on my own. That's
okay. It has to be, otherwise I'll lose myself. I
can't be the wreck I was back then. Sobbing
in sluice rooms, hurting so much. So damned
much. I'd thought we were a team, you know? I
thought we belonged…no, I thought *I* belonged.
But I don't. So, I have to be a team of one.' She
stared up at him, eyes shining. 'You know, when
I was falling down the mountain and I thought
I was going to die I saw Isla's face, Odin's, too,
and yours, Matthieu. But not my parents' faces.
Or even David's. That must tell you a lot. I've
left them behind, they're no longer part of me or
my life.'

She'd thought about him in extremis. About
her life here and not about what she'd endured
before. He tried not to read too much into that.
Had she pushed her traumas so far down she be-

lieved she'd dealt with them? Because she was fooling herself. Even he could see they marred her thoughts and actions still. Everyone she'd loved had let her down. God knew what it was going to take for her to truly trust again.

He knew he couldn't change what had happened to her, but he wanted to make her feel better now. He wanted to show Rachel that she mattered, that he saw her, that he knew her. That her present and her future needn't be marred by her past.

But then, what did he know about that? His past coloured everything he did. So, he was probably setting them both up to fail, but he wanted, so badly, to try. For her.

He stroked her cheek. 'You can rely on me, Rachel Tait.'

'Oh, Matthieu. You're a good man and I know you mean it.' Her smile was genuine and warm and she covered his hand. 'But I don't want to rely on anyone, can't you see? I've learnt that there's no point setting yourself on a course for heartbreak. We've only got ourselves, in the end, right? That's why we just need to have some fun. Nothing heavy.'

He had a bad feeling that heavy was exactly the route he was taking, whether either of them wanted it or not. 'Sounds like we've both got pretty messed-up family history, *chérie*.'

'Doesn't everyone?' She laughed. 'And it's up

to us to survive it. I used to put on my headphones and listen to loud music so I couldn't hear them fight. Then dance round my bedroom until I felt better.'

'The terrible music you were listening to when you were skiing that first time?' At her bugged eyes he said with a grin, 'I heard you. I think the whole resort heard you.'

'Good, I hope they smiled. Better still, joined in. But, Matthieu, how can you say that? Eighties rock anthems are not terrible, they saved my life. Or my sanity at least.' She raised her hands above her head and rocked from side to side, dancing to a beat only she could hear. 'You should try it. Pass me my phone. I'll find some music and I'll show you.'

'Mine's here.'

She scrolled through his music app and grinned. 'Come on, raise your hands... Ready? Final Countdown! Now, sing as loudly as you can.'

He almost did, but couldn't quite bring himself to do it. Besides, he was far too busy watching her. 'It's the middle of the night, Rachel.'

'So? We're far enough away from anyone. No one will hear.'

'And I'm stone-cold sober. Men only dance when they're drunk.' Not that he hadn't frequented clubs, only he'd been happier to watch from the sidelines—basically, the bar—and let the celebs and his friends strut their stuff on the dance floor.

'Ha! No way.' She laughed. 'Real men dance sober, too. And I've got a busted knee and a very sore back, but I'm determined not to let that stop me having fun.'

'Still…' He held his hand up for a definite no.

'Oh. You probably know the singers? You probably went on holiday with them and think I'm the very opposite of cool.' She grinned. 'My love for ballet turned into a love for music. The louder the better as far as I'm concerned and for dancing any old way. My kind of dancing. And I don't care.'

She really didn't, he could see that. She didn't try to be anyone she wasn't. She didn't crave fame or wealth, she just wanted to be accepted for who she was. That would be enough for her.

Thing was, Matthieu didn't just accept her, he wanted her…with a force he'd never felt before. As if he'd die if he didn't sink into her again and pretty damned soon. But he held it together. 'No, I didn't holiday with the band. And I don't want you to be cool. I prefer you hot and getting hotter.'

'Then warm me up, Matthieu.' She put her arms round his neck and swayed with him— standing on her one good leg, singing the words and wriggling her hips until he couldn't do anything but join in.

She did this to fill the gaps, to cover the silence. She danced to a song no one else could hear. She entertained herself, shut out the world. Chose to be alone, whereas he surrounded himself with people, friends, women, work. But, in the end he and Rachel were the same: two people trying to deal with the past in any way they knew how. Trying to find meaning and get through.

Hell, getting through would be a lot better if he did it with Rachel Tait, especially if they spent their time doing this.

He swayed with her, twirled her round…or rather, helped her hop in a circle. Sang what scant lyrics he knew…not loudly to start with, but as embarrassment slunk away he raised his voice and he had to admit she was right; it did make everything better.

She laughed, encouraging him along, and he felt the ache in his chest start to loosen, the slip and slide of her mouth against his as she sang the words between snatched kisses. The play of her hands in his. This serious, beautiful, buttoned-up doctor was also a spirited woman who had so much to give, was sexier than hell and drove him crazy with desire.

He watched her flipping her hair from side to side, the graceful way she moved her hips, the swish of her perfect breasts in her too-big-for-her robe and was utterly transfixed. Enchanted. *Captured.* His heart, his body. He was hers. Completely.

He pulled her to him and kissed her and she

gyrated against him, making him hard and hot. Harder and hotter than ever before. And before he could stop himself, he was pulling her down on to the bed, sheathed and sliding into her.

'Yes, Matthieu. Yes. Yes.' Her kisses became frantic and intense, her moans the only soundtrack he could hear. She grasped at his skin, fingernails digging deep into his shoulders. He thrust inside her over and over, driven by a wild unstoppable need, sinking deeper and harder, feeling her tighten around him, holding him there. Every stroke melded his heart to her. Every kiss forged their connection tighter and stronger.

She moaned, moving her hips with his, never once breaking eye contact. He threaded his fingers into hers, arms above her head, his gaze latched tight to hers. Those grey eyes holding a glimmer of trust and a lot of want. And something else, too, something he didn't want to put a name to.

Then she said his name on a sob, and he found his release...and it felt as if something inside him broke open, all the heavy and all the light mingling together, all the stars in the sky, the whole Milky Way, bunching tight in his heart, in a Rachel-shaped space.

## CHAPTER FOURTEEN

HE WAS GONE by the time she woke up.

She blinked into a room filled with sunlight. He'd opened the curtains, left a tray with hot chocolate and croissants. Sent a text:

Call me when you wake up and I'll come over to help you. xx

Not that any of that made up for his absence because she missed him already. He'd taken her to heights she'd never known existed before, kissed her in a way she'd never been kissed. And she really, *really* wanted to do it all again.

But it did give her time to think.

Last night—this morning—had been more intense than anything she'd ever experienced. She'd decided to be fun and to seduce him, yet he'd teased her history from her bit by painful bit, like picking petals from an ox-eye daisy. Tug and release. Tug and release, on and on, until there was nothing about her he didn't know. She'd exposed her past like a raw nerve.

She'd expected him…okay, she hadn't known

what to expect from him, because she'd never said words like *humiliation* or *belong* about herself before, never admitted to wanting to be a daddy's girl, so she'd thought he might be shocked, but not *moved*. He'd looked as if he was living her pain. And while it had felt wonderful to have someone share the hurt, she didn't want to expect that from him, to think that could be something permanent in her life.

She wanted sex, yes—and lots more with Matthieu—but preferably not with the accompaniment of equilibrium-knocking emotions that she had spent her life trying to avoid. She was a grown woman, a medical professional and that was who she wanted to convey to everyone and especially to Matthieu. Not someone looking to belong to anyone. She was done with all that.

*Had* been done with that.

After showering and dressing she used her ski poles to help her hop over to reception to organise a taxi to take her for her scan. But she stopped short as her eyes were drawn to the biggest fir tree she'd ever seen and to the beautiful man dressing it with Christmas decorations.

He grinned as she hopped over, striding to greet her with a kiss on each cheek. 'Good morning, Rachel.'

Her heart danced and her body keened towards him, which she was fairly sure was obvious to anyone who looked at her, so she quickly scanned the room to make sure no one was listening, but they were all engrossed in their own jobs. She felt weirdly shy around him, not knowing how to be that professional woman when the second she was in his company she just wanted to step into his embrace and stay there. 'Hi, Matthieu. How's the medical centre going?'

He kept his hand on her arm. Protective. Possessive. 'Suzanne's coping and Eric is coming in early to cover for you.'

'I feel so bad not being up there pulling my weight.'

'We can work something out. Scan first. Wait—' He dashed across the reception hall, grabbed her a chair, then made her sit in it. 'How do you feel?'

'Truthfully? Like I was broken into pieces and then put back together.' She smiled up at him, because she couldn't help herself. But *broken*? She never said things like that. She needed to stop thinking like that.

But he didn't seem put off by her gushing, he just grinned and stroked his thumb over her mouth. Their secret shining in his eyes. 'A good sleep can do that.'

*So can good sex.*

'Thanks for letting me have a lie-in.'

'You were exhausted.' His smile told her that he knew exactly why and he very much wanted to share his bed with her again. 'You should have called. I'd have come over to get you.'

And let him see her struggle? No way. Being looked after last night was enough of a dent to her ego. She was a capable woman and wanted him to see her as one. 'I'm fine. I can do this weird shuffle-hop thing with the help of two poles and some decent painkillers. I was just about to organise transport to the hospital for the scan.'

He frowned. 'I'll take you.'

'Honestly, I can manage.' She looked up at the half-dressed Christmas tree. Hundreds of little silver lights flickered behind glittery baubles in myriad colours. 'It looks like you're busy.'

'A little. But if you help me, we can finish it quickly, then I'll drive you into town.' He handed her a gold bauble. 'Find a place for this, please.'

'Bossy.' She laughed. 'Where?'

'Anywhere you want. You choose.'

'Be careful what you wish for. The only bonus of living in two houses was that I always had two Christmas trees to dress. So, you've asked an expert.' She hung the bauble on the tree as warmth spread through her. This was so domesticated and so intimate.

And there…right there, her thoughts started to coalesce. It was *too intimate*. Starting to feel like a real relationship. One with expectations and plans. Hopes and dreams. Taking someone into account, second-guessing what they were feeling and wanting. Changing herself to fit into what they wanted. She could too easily fall into that trap again and then where would she be? Back to hurting again.

So many warning alarms rang in her head, but when she looked up at him and saw him beaming down at her she took a deep breath. She was overreacting. After their special night together she was imbuing the whole thing with the issues she'd inherited from her previous break-up. Matthieu wasn't asking for anything more. He was just asking her to hang a bauble on a tree.

She pushed it on to a branch. 'I like symmetry. Baubles matching on each side.'

'I like a big mess of colour.' He strung gold tinsel across the boughs of the tree, then stuck a red bauble next to her gold one. Too close in her opinion. 'We didn't have a tree every year—most years, in fact. But Louis's house always had the biggest and brightest tree in the village, so I used to go over there and help them dress theirs. It almost made up for it.'

She immediately squished her need to match the baubles and let him carry on making a mess even though it made her shudder, just a little. 'Kids continually amaze me. They always find a way to happiness.'

'There's a lesson there. Let's grab some now.' Winking, he came over and crouched down in front of her. It was only then that she realised he'd placed the chair in the corner of the room, out of direct line of sight of anyone. He kissed her full on the lips, then held both her hands. 'I didn't intend for you to end up in my bed when I invited you to stay in my house. But I'm very glad you were there.'

She palmed his cheek, acutely aware they were at work, but choosing to grab a bit of that elusive happiness while she had the chance. She pressed her lips to his again. 'Are you worried about the line we crossed?'

'Not at all. I'm sure we can keep our night together out of the spotlight. I just don't want you to think I was taking advantage of the situation.'

She laughed as she stroked his inner thigh. Yes, this was fine. The man just wanted sex. She could do that. *Wanted* to do that. 'I like to think I seduced you, Matthieu.'

His eyes met hers, suffused with heat. 'And you're doing it again.'

'Just…taking advantage of the situation.' She chuckled, as a matching heat seeped through her. 'It would be rude not to—'

'Matthieu! Matthieu!' A little voice had them jumping apart and turning round.

Rachel craned her neck round the tree to see Isla in a wheelchair being pushed by her father.

Matthieu's eyebrows rose as he quickly squeezed Rachel's hands and let go, then strode to talk to the little girl. He crouched down by the side of her chair giving her a high-five. '*Coucou,* Isla.'

'*Coucou*, Matthieu. *Coucou*, Rachel.'

'Hi, there.' She looked from one to the other. '*Coucou*?'

'It means hi,' Isla chirped. 'Matthieu taught me. And *Joy...eux Noel* means Happy Christmas.' Stumbling over the words she looked at the boss with the kind of adoration Rachel was used to seeing whenever people looked at Matthieu. And her heart tripped again.

Trying to keep things polite although still feeling quite impolite towards him, she nodded to Michael, then beamed at the little girl, raising her leg to show her the knee brace. 'Snap!'

Isla's eyes widened. 'You, too? Did you get knocked over by a snowboarder?'

'No. It was my own silly fault. I fell over and slid down a mountain.' Her eyes darted to Matthieu and she saw the smile on his lips.

Isla nodded seriously. 'Did Matthieu rescue you on the snowmobile?'

'He did.' The whole of Rachel's body blushed as she thought about all the things that had happened between him picking her up off the mountain and now. Hot chocolate kisses, a bathroom seduction, letting him in to her darkest thoughts, naked dancing... All of it filling her up, but as she watched him and ached to be touched by him again, she had a bad feeling it wasn't enough.

Would one night with him be enough? Ten nights? A hundred?

Then she filed all those thoughts away and focused on her patient. 'How's your knee doing, sweetie?'

'Sore. But we're watching lots of movies and Daddy gives me ice-cream and tells me not to tell Mom. And Mom gives me pizza and tells me not to tell Daddy.' Isla grinned as if she'd won the lottery.

But discomfort wormed through Rachel's gut as she glanced at Michael and frowned in question. Had they not learned anything?

His thin mouth broke into a smile. 'It's okay, honestly. Things are good. We had a long chat after you highlighted how we were behaving. Then we cancelled all our commitments over the holidays and decided to stay here for some real family time. Just the three of us. The parent treats play-off is just a game now.'

Rachel would have preferred no play-offs, but she couldn't help smiling, knowing they'd tried to make things better for Isla. But her heart ached, too, wishing she'd had parents who'd been so committed to making things work, or to something even resembling a civilised divorce instead of a battlefield. 'I'm so glad things are working out.'

'Us, too. Thanks for giving us a reality check.

Bianca will be along in a minute. We're heading into town.'

'Hey, Isla, want to help with the tree?' Matthieu handed the little girl a bauble almost as big as her hand, then lifted her up so she could hang it high. Then another and another until the bauble box was empty and there was a gaudy mismatch of colour covering the branches. Rachel's hands itched to put it into some kind of symmetry, but she understood she had to let that go.

She'd let go of a lot of things these past few weeks.

Eventually, Matthieu put Isla back down on the ground. 'There you go, sugar. Every time you come past the tree you can see your beautiful handiwork.'

Rachel was entranced just watching him. The cute faces he pulled to make Isla laugh, the gentle voice, the tender way he helped her hang the decorations. He was a kind, generous man who'd been through so much pain, yet just wanted to make people smile. He deserved so much happiness.

Her eyes pricked. Something hot slid into her chest, like a weird yearning. A need that actually hurt. Was it Isla? Sure, she was as cute as a button. Rachel hadn't ever thought about having kids…at least not since the break-up with David. Of course, they'd idly talked about having them at some point, but there'd never been a plan. And she hadn't realised how much she ached for them. She should have realised that when she'd fallen head over heels for Odin.

Or was it Matthieu she ached for? Matthieu and a child? A family?

*No.* No, she couldn't be so far down the line with him that she was envisioning a future. She couldn't do that to herself. Couldn't let all that resolve go along with everything else. Her heart fluttered in panic as reality dawned: she was way down the line already.

The real problem was, he wasn't asking for more, but she was wanting it.

What was she going to do? She had to pull back, find herself again. Find the bricks of her wall that he'd carefully smashed down kiss by kiss and reconstruct it again, tight and tall around her heart.

'Just gorgeous, Iles. But don't be too long now.' Bianca's voice behind her was filled with softness, in such a contrast to her highly strung tone last week, and, turning to look at her, Rachel saw the transformation in the model's features from pinched and tense to radiant and happy. 'Don't forget we're heading to the hospital for a check-up for that knee.'

Rachel grabbed the opportunity to have some space from Matthieu. 'Oh? Could I please hitch a ride?'

'Why? Have you hurt yourself, too?' Bianca looked her up and down.

'Knee. Yes. Yes, please, a ride to the hospital would be great.'

Had she really just asked these people for a lift? But they were her ticket out of here so she could have some breathing space. She turned to Matthieu, hoping he wasn't going to insist he take her instead. 'Is that okay?'

She realised, too, that she'd asked him instead of telling him, taking him into account even when she was trying to get distance.

'Of course.' He nodded and smiled, but his eyes were filled with questions. 'I've a million things to do. Let me know what the verdict is? Maybe we could have a chat later?'

'Sure.' She smiled, then turned away.

Not even sure what to say.


'The ligament's not torn, but it is badly sprained. Aargh!' Hands fisting, Rachel hopped back and forth on her crutches across her chalet lounge floor, her mouth a taut line. 'I'm so sorry, Matthieu. I know this is going to be a big hassle for you and the team.'

'We'll work something out.' Matthieu bit down on his own frustration that she hadn't been in contact with him for hours and also that the resort now had a less than ideal staffing situation. The latter he could deal with, the former suggested he needed to take a chill pill. She was her own woman. She could go into town and have a scan without him.

Even so, the fact she'd dumped him for a ride with Bianca rankled. Because, more than anything, Rachel didn't like Bianca, and she'd just spent the night with him. *Tant pis.*

She grimaced. 'But I came here to work up the mountain and now I can't even leave the resort without help. I hate letting you down. And being dependent on someone else.'

'You don't say?' He reached for her arm and pulled her down on to his knee on the couch. 'You have to rest and elevate your leg. It isn't going to heal if you keep using it.'

'I know.' She slumped against him, staring wistfully out of the window. 'I should be up there with Suzanne and Eric.'

'They can manage. You can do remote consultations.'

'Sure. We did a lot of video consults when that virus hit a couple of years ago. It's not quite the same though, is it?'

'The same as hands on? Not at all. We like hands on, right?' He leaned in for a kiss. Was it his imagination, or did she tug away far too soon? Probably his imagination. 'I've taken the liberty of setting you up in the office at my lodge. It has the best Wi-Fi in the resort and lots of room for you to have a proper set-up with a desktop computer, large monitor and headset. Trying to fit anything on this tiny dining table would be challenging.'

'Oh. I see. Well… I think it would be better if it was in my space, to be honest.' She pointed to the too-small table. 'I'll make it work.'

'If you like.'

She nodded. 'I just prefer—'

'Your own space.'

'Is that such a bad thing?' She looked spooked. She'd looked spooked earlier, too. Something had shaken her, something to do with Isla. Or was it their night together?

But even though she was probably right—space was a good thing—he liked being around her. Liked having someone to care about, someone to care for him. Liked waking up to her. Talking to her. Sharing. Which was a whole new thing for him and it was all down to Rachel.

But he knew better than to let things get too cosy. 'No, you're right, of course.'

'I'm sorry. I'm tired.' She looked at him for a moment and he saw a hundred different emotions pass through her gaze before she ran her palm over her forehead and sighed. 'And in pain, to be honest, and frustrated that I can't do my job. And I feel guilty that I've let you down.'

'No. Don't ever feel guilty. It was an accident.' He knew guilt coloured everything. She didn't need to add that to her pain and exhaustion. He circled his hands round her waist and pulled her closer. Feeling the hot press of her body against his, the softening of her muscles as she relaxed against him. Eventually. But he did notice the hesitation that hadn't been there last night. 'Get some rest, *chérie*. Have a break and don't put too much pressure on yourself.'

She placed her hands on his chest as if she was about to push away from him, but she didn't. 'I have to work.'

'You have to rest. Damn it, Rachel. Just for an hour or so. You need time out.' He gently slid her off his knee on to the chair and stood up. This was getting them nowhere. 'I'll leave you to it. I'll see you later.'

He started towards the door, but heard her voice behind him. 'No. Wait.'

'What?'

'Look, last night was great. I loved it. But I don't want anyone here to know about it. Not Louis or anyone. I had enough trouble in my last job trying to pick apart my work and my private life.'

'Of course.'

'And I'm not looking for anything serious… you know that. This morning I had a wobble because the whole Christmas tree thing was lovely. And I was still feeling all sexy from our night together and I started to feel…' Her cheeks turned a dark shade of red. 'I don't know… You're fun to be around, Matthieu. But you listen, too. And you're great with kids. It felt cosy by the tree and I decided I shouldn't get used to feeling cosy.'

That word again. That feeling of letting your guard down. 'Things did get intense last night. It was fun, though.'

'Yes. And basically, I just can't seem to stop wanting you.' She ran her fingertips along his jaw. 'What I'm trying to say is, other than that I'm an idiot—'

'You're all about the sex?' He laughed.

'Yes. Yes.' Her shoulders sagged with relief. 'I'm not looking for anything more.'

'Excellent. We're a good match then.' His brain was already working on a rerun of last night, his body more than prepared. Although…even though he agreed with her, he felt deflated, too. Part of him wanted…what did he want? More. Deeper. Which was ridiculous, because he was already embroiled too deeply in this.

'I'm so glad you understand.' She kissed him and this time there was no hesitation.

When she eventually pulled away, he stepped his fingertips over her collarbone. 'I chose the beds for these chalets. I know they're plenty big enough for two.'

She laughed and rubbed her head against his chest. 'What are you thinking, Matthieu?'

'Whether I can take you up on that offer to

strip you naked. Help you relax.' He smoothed his hand over her breast and saw heat mist her gaze.

But she leaned away from him, a small frown forming over her eyes. 'But work…?'

'But first…?' His other hand slid up to her cheek, cupping her face.

'Matthieu.' Her mouth curved into a very sexy smile. 'What are you doing to me?'

'Something good, I hope.' He laughed. 'Let me take care of you.'

'I don't even know what that feels like.' She blinked up at him, eyes glistening.

Her words were like a knife in his gut. She'd had to look after herself, even after the break-up. Or maybe she'd pushed too many people away. People who didn't understand her the way he did. What she needed was time and space and encouragement. He would give her all of those things if it meant he got to know her better. What turned her on, what made her smile. He'd tried hard not to get involved, but he kept coming back for more.

He stroked her hair. 'It's a lot like last night. But way more sex. Let me show you.'

Her hand covered his. 'And then?'

There was so much he could say, so much he could offer, but they'd just agreed this was sex and fun and temporary. 'Then I'll bring the computer over and you can work.'

'Okay.' She licked his bottom lip then sucked it into her mouth. 'That's a very good plan.'

'I'm a planner, what can I say?' He laughed and pulled her closer, put his lips to that tender spot just below her ear. 'I have so much planned for you in the bedroom, too.'

'Matthieu... I can't...think... Yes, please...' Her hands were on each side of his face and she kissed him as if her life depended on it. Kissed him and kissed him until he was left in no doubt about what she wanted from him. At least for now.

And that's what they'd agreed: now was all that mattered.

# CHAPTER FIFTEEN

'HE LOST CONTROL and hit a tree. Head injury. Nasty cut on his forehead.' Matthieu's voice was crackly, and the image kept shorting out, but she could just make out a prone young man, very still with his eyes closed. An open wound oozed blood on to the fresh snow.

'Is he conscious?' Rachel watched the monitor, controlling her frustration that she couldn't be there doing the first responder assessment on the injured snowboarder, having to make do with a screen and a dodgy cellphone network. But it was better than nothing, and this set-up had served them well for the last couple of weeks. On good days Matthieu drove her up to the medical centre on the snowmobile, but this morning she'd had a knee check-up in town, so she'd stayed at the hotel.

It wasn't perfect—she couldn't fully do what she needed to do, but they improvised. Like this: talking them through serious incidents while co-ordinating the emergency response. With a lot of resting with her leg elevated in between.

Matthieu held the digital tablet so she could

see the patient. 'He was responding when we got here, but he's deteriorating quickly.'

Not good. 'If you talk to him, does he open his eyes?'

'Justin? Justin?' Matthieu tapped their patient's face. 'Justin, can you hear me? No.'

'Can you squeeze his nail bed for me? One of his fingers? Any one.'

Matthieu did as she asked. Then shook his head. 'Nothing. But he's maintaining his own airway.'

'Okay.' That was something. Rachel started to tap the landline phone to put a call through for an emergency evacuation. 'It's important we get him out of there as quickly as we can.'

'We'll put a collar on and keep him warm.' Matthieu put his hands at each side of Justin's neck, waiting for Cody to slide the collar on.

'Can you cover that wound up, too, please?' Rachel thought about what more she could do all the way down here. 'Is he with friends or family?'

'No one around but him. But he's holidaying with a group. I don't know where they are. Lucky one of the crew found him.'

God, she wished she was up there helping. Sitting here was driving her insane. 'Leave his helmet on, too. I'm phoning for the air ambulance. What's your location?'

'Just off Heaven's Gate. Near where we found you. I'll text through the GPS co-ordinates.'

'Okay. It can be treacherous up there. Be careful.'

'Thanks, Rachel.' Matthieu looked up into the monitor and smiled. For a brief moment he held her gaze, then he focused back on the injured boarder.

With that one look, her chest heated. Her body heated. Even though this working situation was frustrating, he'd made it as easy as possible for her to contribute. And he'd certainly made her evenings interesting. They'd fallen into a routine of one night at her chalet and one night at his lodge. Their secret. And it had been perfect: fun, sexy, giving and taking.

She smiled back, hoping it was reassuring, but understanding that he knew the dangers up there as well as she did. 'I'll let you know ETA.'

'Great. Looks like the weather's closing in.'

Which would mean delays. 'I'll tell them to get a hurry on.'

'Thanks. Over.' She called it in and waited for the helicopter response. Then took a deep breath before she conveyed her news to Matthieu. 'They said they'd try to reach you, but the potential for icing is high.'

'They can't fly in thick snow. Freezing precipitation stops the blades working. But...we need them here. Quickly. It's not just the head injury I'm worried about, it's frostbite and hypothermia.'

'I'll let them know.'

Then she waited. And waited.

She watched more heavy clouds roll in. Broke the news to Matthieu that the chopper had returned to base, so he and Cody had called extra help to bring blankets and for help lifting Justin if needs be. Eventually, unable to wait any more, they carefully manoeuvred him on to the snowmobile and drove him slowly to the medical centre. Time chugged round from lunchtime to early afternoon. Matthieu's reports were more and more demanding.

*'We need an evacuation now. We need the chopper now. Tell them, Rachel. Tell them to hurry.'*

Then she heard the welcome sound of helicopter rotors and looked out to a clearing sky. 'They're here, Matthieu,' she told him. 'How's he doing?'

'Not good.' His tone was flat. 'He's warm and safe, but that's the best we can do.'

When he arrived back at the hotel with Cody an hour later, they both looked frozen through and ashen. She ushered them into her chalet and gave them hot drinks, wrapped them in thick wool blankets…wanting to wrap Matthieu into her arms, too, but holding back. 'How was he?'

'He was in a bad way, Rachel. He was still breathing when the helicopter took off, but I don't know if he'll make it.' Matthieu shrugged. He was so pale and cold it made Rachel's heart twist. 'On

Christmas Eve, too. I'll inform his family and arrange for them to get here as soon as I can. We managed to catch up with his friends on our way down the mountain. They've gone to the hospital.'

'Is he a local?' She prayed he wasn't, because she knew the delayed evacuation would have serious impact on Justin's condition. Even worse if he was Matthieu's friend. She knew he still carried guilt over not being able to save his mother and someone else dying on his watch would weigh heavily on him.

He smiled softly. 'Justin is a very famous American singer and songwriter, with a string of hits and lots of awards.'

'So, his family will have a long way to travel before they can see him.'

Matthieu nodded. Having got used to her inability to recognise a star, he never mentioned his surprise now. 'I'll get them here as quickly as I can.'

Cody stood. 'I'm heading for a shower, then a drink in the bar. Fancy joining me for a beer?'

'Sure. I need something strong after that.' Matthieu stood, too, folding the blanket neatly and putting it on the couch. 'I need to debrief the staff anyway. But first I have to make those calls.'

'You coming, too, Doc?' Cody hovered at the door. 'It's always better to deal with things like this as a team.'

'Yes. Thanks, I will.' She liked that he thought

she was part of their team even though she couldn't do her job as well as she might. 'I'll call the hospital for an update first.' Which of course was only a little elaboration. She just wanted some alone time with Matthieu.

After watching Cody go, she gave Matthieu a hug. 'You okay?'

He was still cold. He looked haunted, his features hollowed out. 'I hate it when we can't help them.'

'You did help. You kept him warm and safe. That's all anyone could do until the chopper arrived. You may have saved his life.' It wasn't that she'd got used to it in her line of work…losing anyone was hard…but it was something she did experience in the emergency room. What amazed her was that Matthieu was okay about admitting these things. Usually, in this situation she'd just tell everyone she was fine and bury those feelings deep, but here he was saying them out loud. Just being his amazing self, he'd taught her a lot about her own issues.

He raised his palms. 'It could all be too late. I would have flown that damned helicopter myself if I could have.'

'You did what you could. It's not your fault that the weather closed in.' She put her arms around his neck and held him, wishing she could take away his pain. Knowing that today's helplessness mingled with memories of him finding his mum.

'You did your best, Matthieu. That's all anyone can ever ask of you.'

'What if it isn't enough? What if I could have done more? What if I should have tried harder?' Doubt swamped his features. But she knew what he was really asking. Had he done enough for his mother? Had he missed anything? Could he have saved her?

She didn't know the answer to that, but she believed, beyond a shadow of a doubt, that there was nothing more Matthieu could have done to save the life of someone so determined to end it. So, she held him tight and whispered, 'One thing I've learnt in the ER is that sometimes bad things happen and we can't stop them, no matter how hard we try. You can't blame yourself when you absolutely do your best and when someone's too far gone to save them. You, Matthieu LeFevre, care enough to try…harder than anyone else. This is not your fault. You are enough. You are enough.'

He held on, too, silent and drawn. Her heart ached for him and she wanted, so much, to be able to carry his pain, carry all of the team's pain.

No. Carry Matthieu's pain.

The last few weeks she'd learnt so much from him: how to relax more, how to share, how to give. How to receive more, too. How to be a friend, a lover. How to care for someone. Properly care. Put their needs ahead of your own. Like Matthieu did, continually for other people. For her.

The connection between them had tightened and something had bloomed inside her, something deep and resonant and strong.

And as she held him, her heart swelled with so many more complex emotions. Sexual desire, sure. That was always present when she was with Matthieu. But this desire…this need to erase his pain and to wish him only the most wonderful of lives, this ache she carried when he wasn't around, the excitement when he was. It threatened to overwhelm her.

It was like nothing she'd experienced before. It was pure and bright and possessive and passionate. It was raw and savage, yet soft and yielding. She hadn't felt it for her ex. Not like this…so *much* of it all the time.

Matthieu nuzzled against her neck, still holding her as if she was his lifeline. 'Thank you, Rachel. I needed that. I needed you. I hope that's okay?'

'Of course. I want you to talk to me about these things. Don't ever feel you can't.' But she wasn't sure how to deal with being needed and how that made her light up inside. She wanted to hold him for ever, never wanted this closeness to end. Even though she knew it would, because something this good never lasted. 'Just…tell me you don't blame yourself. Please.'

He blinked. Then looked away. She pulled him to look at her. His pain torturing her. 'Listen to me. It wasn't your fault. You fought and you fought. You can't save everyone, Matthieu, hard as that is. And you can't lose yourself in the aftermath. It's not fair to spend the rest of your life feeling guilty for something you couldn't stop happening. Sadly…oh, so sadly, it was going to happen anyway. You'd say that to Cody, you'd say it to me, or Louis, and you have to say it to yourself. So, say it.'

Moments passed. He swallowed. Blinked. Then fixed on her gaze. 'It…wasn't my fault.'

'Oh, Matthieu.' She hugged him, her throat a raw mess of unshed tears. 'I'm so proud of you.'

Eventually, he unfolded himself from her arms and stroked her cheek. Back to his wonderful, commanding self. 'It's Christmas Eve, we need some festive cheer.'

'You go. I'll be over in a minute.' She tried to breathe out. Tried to calm herself. Because she knew what this was, this muddle of extreme emotion. And it was wondrous and yet terrifying at the same time.

She'd fallen in love with him. Or at least, was falling hard and fast and irrevocably.

And that wasn't just one of those silly personal mistakes she kept on making, it was a monumental disaster.

The bar was decorated with so much tinsel and twinkling Christmas lights it made Rachel blink and wish she'd put her sunglasses on. The log fire

crackled and hissed in the corner, laughter ema-
nated from groups huddled around tables. Christmas songs played in the background and there
was a fizzy feeling in the air, of excitement and
anticipation. A typical Christmas Eve.

She found Matthieu and the others sitting
around a large table in the far corner, out of the
way of the paying guests. She dug deep for a
smile. 'Hey.'

'Doc! Come sit down. Here's a glass of your
favourite.' Zoe scooted up to make space for Rachel who hop-shuffled into the seat between the
receptionist and Matthieu. A glass of merlot sat
in front of her on the table.

'Wow. Love the service. Thank you.'

Zoe, Matthieu, Louis and two of the lift hands
all began jeering as Cody tried to extricate a
wooden brick from the middle of a tower on the
table.

'Hey. Any news on Justin?' Matthieu said quietly. As always, his manner with her was friendly,
but not too intimate, when they were in company. Truth was, she didn't want to sit so close
to him now she'd had her revelation and actually
acknowledged her feelings.

She refused to love him. She refused to love
anyone. And even if she had developed feelings,
she would bury them deep inside her and pretend
they weren't there. 'They've managed to stabi-
lise him and he's having brain scans at the mo-

ment. They'll have more news for us tomorrow. I'll chase it up in the morning.'

'Thanks.'

'You want to have a general debrief?'

'That's what I'd planned.' Matthieu looked round the laughing group. 'But not at the moment. Cody was the one most shaken up and he seems okay. If he brings it up we can talk it through. Let him have fun for now.'

'Okay. Hopefully, we'll be able to give him good news tomorrow.'

'In the meantime, we put on a happy face for the guests and staff for Christmas Day, too.' He looked troubled, but determined not to let it overtake him. 'You want to join in Jenga?'

'Yes!' Louis clapped, clearly having already had a fair amount of Christmas spirit. 'You can be on our team, Rach.'

'No.' Zoe held up her hand. 'She's sitting next to me, she can be on my team.'

'Hey, don't fight over me.' Rachel's chest glowed.

Despite her misgivings about her feelings for Matthieu she found herself laughing, feeling valued and part of something. This was what she wanted, right? To be part of the team. Having friends. Not to have fallen in love with Matthieu thrown into the mix.

He was so close, she could feel the brush of his arm against hers and even now ached for his hands on her. She closed her eyes briefly, pushing it all further down inside. 'Looks like the teams have even numbers at the moment. I'll join in next round.'

She watched as they all took turns to tease out a brick, the emotional fallout of Justin's accident easing a little with the camaraderie. Another round of drinks was bought, another game of Jenga played. This time she did join in and enjoyed the banter, even if her team, consisting of herself, Zoe and Matthieu, lost.

Then the hum of conversation settled as they dived into a new round of drinks. Presently, Cody asked, 'So, are we all set for tomorrow? Fancy dress outfits sorted? All our elves and fairies present and correct? How's Santa feeling? Going to be up all night?'

Matthieu blinked. 'Making presents, you mean?'

'Sure.' Louis winked. 'If that's what you want to call it.'

'Everything is wrapped and ready.' Matthieu shook his head, frowning, but ignoring the innuendo. 'Some of the kids get a bit shy in the spotlight, so I'm going to need some help with handing the gifts out.'

'Oh? Aren't you Santa's little helper, Rachel?' Louis laughed, his eyes wide and bright.

A hum of unease settled across Rachel's chest, but she ignored it. Louis was always making silly comments. But Zoe was laughing, Cody, too.

'I… Um… I…' Her eyes darted to Matthieu

for clues on how to respond, but he didn't look at her. She looked back to the others, feeling just as shy as those little kids, with the glare of everyone's gazes on her. 'Happy to help you all out. Any time.' She put emphasis on the *all*.

'But especially Mattie.' Louis laughed. 'Come on, seriously? Did you think we didn't know? It's great news. It's about time Mattie found someone.'

Zoe nudged her. 'It's lovely. Matt deserves some happiness after everything he's been through. We're so pleased for you both.'

'Cheers to the lovebirds.' Cody grinned and raised his glass at them in salutation.

So much for having a secret. Everyone knew.

Rachel's world tilted, the ground beneath her quicksand-soft. She felt completely exposed. As if she'd just walked across the bar naked. As if they could all see her hopes and dreams written on her face and knew her deepest wishes. As if they could see the light she had for Matthieu that was burning brighter and brighter every second she spent with him. And that they knew…because everyone could see, everyone knew, that it was all out of reach for her. She wasn't enough. She was fooling herself that she could have what she wanted.

Because why would she get it now, when she'd never had it before?

They were laughing. Matthieu was silent. He

didn't look at her, but he didn't say anything to contradict Louis either. He just let the comments hang.

So much for being part of a team and having friends. These people weren't her friends, they were his friends. This was his team. Had been before she arrived and would be after she left. She was reliving everything she'd run away from. Worse, their secret felt tarnished, sullied.

And the sad truth was, she loved him and she couldn't bury that any more. It kept bubbling up inside her and threatening to show itself in her mannerisms, her tone, her gaze. It was ever present. All. The. Time.

When would she ever learn?

Her hands felt clammy and her breath caught in her tight chest. The walls were pressing in on her, faces, too…the same way they had when she'd walked down the aisle without a husband.

She had to get out. Air. Space.

'Um. Right. That's me done.' Her cheeks burned as she jumped up and started to shuffle out in front of a baffled-looking Zoe. 'I'm going to get an early night.'

'But you haven't finished your drink.' Zoe tapped Rachel's hand.

'I'm done. Thanks.' And she was. Completely done. This thing was done. It had to be. She didn't want to be gossip, or the subject of innuendo. She didn't want complications at work. She didn't

want to be in love with Matthieu, or with anyone. She didn't want to be wanting permanent or
for ever with someone when it was never going
to happen.

Tears stung her eyes as she hopped on her
crutches towards the exit, ungainly and uncoor-
dinated, wishing she could run, instead of limp-
ing off with all these eyes watching her.

Wishing she hadn't let herself fall so hard in
so many ways.

Wishing she'd never met Matthieu LeFevre,
never mind lost her heart to him.

# CHAPTER SIXTEEN

HE FOUND HER in the barn, sitting on the dusty floor wrapped around Odin and he knew, just by her slumped posture, that he should have left her alone. But he'd been compelled to come find her.

'*Coucou,* Rachel.'

'Matthieu.' Her flat tone was enough warning for more anxiety to slither into his chest. Bloody Louis. A best friend knew when to joke and when to shut up. But then, Louis didn't know anything, he just thought he did. He didn't know about the deal Matthieu had with Rachel. That it was all about the sex. And that it was so much more than that.

She'd pushed him so hard into a corner that he'd had to face the fact he'd been letting guilt run his life. She'd held him as if he mattered. He'd trusted her with his fears. He'd relished her kisses and lovemaking.

Simply, being with her was the best thing in his life.

And feeling that scared the life out of him.

He slid down the wall and sat next to her, his heart a mangled mess, because here he was, trying to read her micro expressions all over again. Wanting to read her mind, to be wrapped in her, in his sheets, rather than watching her wrap herself round his dog like it was some sort of shield. 'You hot-footed it out of the bar and I went to look for you. I figured if you weren't in your chalet, you'd be here with pretty boy. I just want to make sure you're okay.' He didn't even have to explain why. He'd seen the humiliation on her face.

She looked at him, eyes the colour of molten pewter shining with tears. 'Not okay at all.'

'What? No *I'm fine*?' As a joke it was lame, but it gave him an insight into her psyche. She could tell him her feelings now, that was good. Even if those feelings were used against him.

'I'm not fine, Matthieu.' Her voice snapped on *fine* so he put his hand on her arm, just wanting to touch her and help soothe whatever it was that hurt.

'What's wrong?'

She hugged Odin to her chest. 'Everyone was laughing. They all know about us.'

'They just think they do.'

Her eyes blazed now. 'You didn't say anything to shut them up.'

'What could I say? You asked me not to say anything to them about it. I couldn't deny or admit anything.' He'd been stuck between a rock and a hard place, so he'd held back. 'Besides, it's not the worst thing in the world if people know we've got something going on. They were happy for us.'

'I've been here before, remember? I know what the fallout is like. Gossip, innuendo. Talk. When it ends there'll be the dissection of whose friend is whose. And, when it comes down to it, they're all yours. And I'll be alone. Again. Which is fine when I choose it, but not when I have it thrust on me because of a break-up. I like these people, Matthieu. I like this team. I don't want to be marginalised or looking on social media to see what kind of fun you're having without me.' She shook her head vehemently. 'We should never have started this.'

'But we did and we could just carry on having fun and to hell with everyone else.' But he didn't feel as though it was just fun—she was right, it was more than that. It was everything. Intimate, sexy…terrifying.

'It's…the thing is…' She took a deep breath, her bottom lip wavering on the inhale. 'Oh, Matthieu, I've done something really stupid.'

'I doubt that very much. What did you do?'

'You really don't want to know.' She shook her head and nuzzled Odin's fur, looking forlorn and wretched.

His heart pumped like a rifle shot. He wasn't sure he did want to know, but he needed to hear. 'Try me?'

Another deep breath. 'Despite what we agreed,

I know deep in my heart that I do want to be an us. I want the team to know that we're doing… whatever it is we're doing, because I want it to last. I don't want to sneak around, I want to stay around and that's crazy. We agreed. I agreed. This…' She pointed to her heart. 'This is not me. None of it makes sense. And yet it makes complete sense.' Shock ran through her gaze. 'I've fallen for you, Matthieu. I didn't want to, I tried not to, but there it is. Give me a bit longer here and I have a bad feeling I might fall in love with you.'

'Okay.' He thought of all the things he could reply, but they bundled up in his chest.

'And I don't want to. I can't. I just can't.' She gently moved Odin from her legs and clambered to standing, favouring her bad leg, putting her hand on the wall to steady herself. 'It's too hard. Too quick. Too much. I like you too much.'

She loved him, but didn't want to.

Now he wished he hadn't got her to open up. He didn't want love. He didn't want to love anyone.

And he had a bad feeling he was already halfway there, too. And then what? Heartache. Disaster. She'd leave. Trash his heart. Everyone left, one way or another.

He stood, too, trying to settle his tumultuous thoughts, having given up on settling his emotions. 'We agreed it wouldn't get serious.'

Pointless words when his body was aching for her. When the centre of his chest felt as if it was on fire.

'I know.' She smiled sadly and it damned near pierced his heart. 'Silly me. But I couldn't help it. You're so thoughtful and kind. And you kiss… well, you kiss so well. And you listen and you see me. And I thought I could lock my feelings away like I've always done, but I can't stop them coming to the surface. And I don't want them to. I don't want to feel them. I want to be the Ice Queen. Untouchable. I like living like that. Not like this. With too much inside.' She hugged her arms round her chest. 'We need to stop it all and go back to just working together. I'm sorry, Matthieu.'

'You want me to forget the last few weeks and you want me to be okay about it?' He didn't know how to navigate this. Couldn't reconcile this feeling inside him. He should have been relieved, but he felt broken, as if his chest was imploding.

Her eyes closed for a second and she looked as if she was struggling to hold herself together. 'You don't get a choice.'

Yeah. Figured. His life on repeat.

But she was right about falling in love; that could never happen. He'd avoided it for the last few years, giving relationships a wide berth, not allowing anyone to get close. So why he'd let his guard down with Rachel Tait he didn't know. She was so locked up, almost impenetrable. Worse, she didn't *want* to love him.

Maybe that had been the challenge?

Whatever, it didn't matter why he'd let his guard down he had, over and over and now she'd said she could fall in love with him and that fleetingly had made everything brighter. Because he knew those fledgling emotions were seeded inside him, too.

Before he could stop himself, the words tumbled out on one last high of hope. 'What if…what if we tried to navigate a way through this?'

'How?' Desolation flickered in her expression. 'How do we do this without getting closer?'

'I don't know. I just know we can't give up.'

'I just did, Matthieu.'

'We can work it out.' He didn't want to sound desperate, but maybe he could convince her? To what? To stay just to make him feel better? He didn't want that.

'I can't do it.' She shook her head. 'I told you. I can't be part of a couple.'

'You just weren't good at being part of a couple with David.'

'I'm sorry.' She leaned in and kissed his cheek, then slid her arms into her crutches and worked her way towards the door.

'But Rachel… Rachel!' He strode towards her,

but she tugged the door open and slipped out into the freezing night.

'Don't follow me, Matthieu, please. I can manage.'

The familiar cloak of hopelessness fitted itself around him. 'But—'

'No.' She pressed her lips together, but he could see her mouth trembling as if she was holding in a sob. 'Please. Matthieu. Please don't touch me. I'm *fine*.'

And with that he knew he'd lost her.

She hadn't made another mistake, she hadn't. Cutting things off with Matthieu was the best idea.

She'd never wanted a big love and now…she had a bad feeling she'd found one and it was just what she'd imagined. It hurt. Physically hurt. So damned much.

Tears kept welling up and as soon as she fisted them away more came. She couldn't stop them no matter how much she told herself she'd done the right thing. Her body disagreed. Her heart was staging its own revolution.

She hobbled back to the chalet, hoping he wasn't following her, but wishing he was. Wishing he'd try to convince her to go back to his bed. Crazy.

This falling in love thing made no sense. Every step she took away from him made her heart splinter just a little bit more. The crazier thing was, he'd looked at her as if he felt the same way. As if he wanted her as much as she wanted him. *We can work it out.*

She'd almost wavered then. Almost said yes, let's try.

But it wouldn't work out. It had never worked out, not with her parents, not with David, so why would Matthieu be any different? She'd be left with a broken heart. Just like every time she'd tried to love someone.

And this time she didn't know if she'd have the strength to fix it.


It looked as though this Christmas was going to be one of the difficult ones. He'd thought he'd seen the back of those when his mother died, but, no. Here he was, Father Christmas, feeling the least Christmassy he'd ever felt. Feeling more alone than he'd ever felt.

Next year he'd go to the beach, somewhere exotic, and get very drunk.

Sure, the hotel lounge looked amazing. The ice swan centrepiece on the table was magnificent. The tree was magical. The long lunch had been delicious and he'd been surrounded by friends. It was the kind of Christmas he'd always dreamed of. Only, two people were missing.

One he'd never get back, he would only ever have memories, but the other woman was just…

absent. God knew where she was. At least with an injured knee she wouldn't be solo skiing.

Over the last few hours he'd gone over and over what they'd shared together, the things she'd said in the barn. And the things she hadn't said. He knew it had taken so much for her to admit her feelings and he'd been too stupid or scared to accept them warmheartedly. He didn't want to love or be loved. Love wasn't enough.

But he did want her.

'*Père Noël!*' A chorus of screeches.

For now, the fate of Christmas was solely in his hands.

He walked towards the group of children sitting by the tree, the sack of bulging gifts over his shoulder, not feeling at all in the mood, but when he saw the pure joy on their faces he hauled on a grin of his own.

'*Père Noël!*'

Cheering, the kids gathered round and he tried his best to be the Father Christmas they wanted. It didn't take long to hand out the gifts and soon he had the last one in his hands. He sought out the recipient. 'And last, but not at all least, Isla!'

'*Merci,* Matthieu,' she whispered, taking the present in both hands and rewarding him with a huge smile.

'Ahem… *Père Noël*, please.' He winked, really feeling the smile he was giving her instead of just faking it.

'I know it's you, Matthieu.' She laughed and hopped back to her mother's open arms. The little unit of three seemed genuinely happy.

He looked at Michael and Bianca. Against so many odds and dealing with two super-egos they'd found a way to make things work, thanks to Rachel. By not accepting anything but what the little girl deserved she'd made a huge change in Isla's life and in her parents' marriage.

Pain sliced through him. He wished she was here to see this, to be part of this.

He missed her more than he'd thought possible. An ache he knew would never ease. A future he hadn't known he'd wanted had been snatched away from him. A future with her in it and possibly some kids of their own. Hell, he hadn't ever thought about it and he missed it already.

She'd be a fierce and protective mother, a challenging wife…in a good way…pushing them to strive for the best they could be. She would love hard.

Love.

He'd believed for so long that love was the problem; he'd rejected intimacy because love hadn't worked for him. It hadn't stopped his mother taking her life and it couldn't bring her back. It had just caused him a lifetime of pain.

But his mother had made the choice she'd made. He hadn't been able to stop her and guilt for his failure was the burden he carried. But Rachel was right; he'd saved her twice and fought for her for thirty-one years. He'd done his best to love her and she'd known she was loved until the very end. She'd been so determined, and so unhappy, that there'd always been the chance he wouldn't save her. Sometimes you just can't. Maybe she'd hung around a few extra years just to make sure he'd be okay. And he had been, with the help of his friends and this community.

*Love.*

Rachel told him that was what Sainte Colette had given him. It had helped him thrive and nurtured him. Looking back, that's what he'd tried to give them in return, by setting up this resort to give them jobs and a future. It occurred to him... no, it hit him with a force, that love had brought so many positives into his life. And he'd embraced it for a community, but hadn't thought he deserved it, or had been too damned scared to take it for himself. He'd closed himself off from intimacy out of fear. But he knew, rationally, that whatever had been going on with his mother hadn't been because he wasn't enough, it had been because she was ill and couldn't see a way through.

He'd poured all his love for his mother into this place and into his friends. Maybe now it was time to pour all his love into himself. Into a relationship?

To save himself and forge a new future.

There was only one person he wanted to share that with.

He realised then what he'd known all along, but had refused to acknowledge: he didn't just want a future without Rachel in it. He loved her.

He loved her. Yeah. That was a low blow given she didn't want him. Didn't want to love him.

But maybe, if they could put the fear aside and just talked, if he told Rachel what he felt instead of hiding from it, just maybe they could find a way.

He tugged on his ski boots, promising himself he'd find her as soon as the ski show was over.

She didn't want him to save her, but he might just have to try to save himself and convince her to come along for the ride.

# CHAPTER SEVENTEEN

HER HEART WAS breaking so badly she'd hidden away from the festivities, but she wanted to see the show.

With the aid of Bianca and Michael she'd hobbled on to the chairlift and up to the ski field and now stood with them and Isla whooping as elves, fairies, angels and reindeer skied down the slopes doing acrobatics that seemed to defy gravity, to a soundtrack of Christmas songs blaring through loudspeakers. Rachel looked around and saw the magic in everyone's faces and wished she could feel it for herself.

But she was too sad right now. Maybe next year, on a beach, a cocktail in her hand, she'd celebrate Christmas, but not today. Not when her heart hurt so much.

Next to her Bianca and Michael shared a kiss, then a hug with their daughter. They looked happy. Really, genuinely happy. And she hoped it would last.

She hadn't ever wanted what her parents had had, that destructive force and passion, she'd been happy just to be part of something. To share a kiss on Christmas Day with someone who mattered, with someone who cared for her. Someone who thought she mattered too.

Poor David. She'd thought he was the answer. Thought jumping into a marriage with him would protect her from all that hurt, that she'd be content to be content. He clearly hadn't been. He'd wanted more…and who could blame him in the end? Because deep, caring, proper big love was wonderful. It was everything.

Until it ended.

She'd ended it with Matthieu because it had been growing, deepening, becoming a big love for her and she hadn't been able to trust her judgement a second time. Neither of them had wanted more, so it had only been a matter of time before Matthieu ended it anyway. That's what she told herself.

A jingle of bells had her scanning the slopes and she held her breath, waiting for Matthieu to appear. Then there he was, dressed in his red suit and white beard, flying through the air to raucous cheers and applause.

She watched as he whooshed down the hill, then on to the rail for a jump. She held her breath again as he soared high, doing the splits mid-air, then landing.

Wobbled. Righted himself. *No.*

He wobbled again, then slid sideways, falling, tumbling down the hill towards the barrier.

Everyone stopped talking. All she could hear was the tinny music and the sound of her heart rushing in her ears. He was falling and falling and falling. Then he stopped.

*Get up. Get the hell up.*

But he didn't move.

*Come on, Matthieu. Please.*

Nothing.

*No. Matthieu. Please. No.*

*We can work it out.* He'd given her a lifeline with those words, a chance to talk things through. To be honest about what they wanted and felt. To be together. To trust each other with secrets and pain and to help each other heal. And she'd been so scared by what she was feeling she'd panicked. Rejected him.

He still didn't move.

*Matthieu.*

*Ray Shell.*

All the love and truth she'd been hiding from hit her then like a thunderbolt. What if she never got the chance to tell him properly how she felt? What if it was too late? What if all her second-guessing had stopped her having the best thing she could ever have in her life? Matthieu LeFevre. Her big love of a lifetime.

No. She couldn't lose him. Wouldn't.

'Matthieu! No!' She pushed her way through the crowd, wincing at every painful step as she hobbled across the snow. When she reached him, he was being attended to by an elf and a reindeer she recognised as Cody. 'Let me through. Please.'

She fell to her knees and touched his face, then closed her eyes and pressed her mouth to his. Felt the shudder of breath against her lips. But he didn't kiss her back. 'Are you okay? Please be okay.'

'Hey, there.' Blue eyes blinked up at her. His hand went to her trembling lips, but she grasped his fingers.

It was fear, she knew. For both of them. Fear of getting hurt. Fear of rejection. Fear of letting someone in. But hell, if he could fly down that mountain without a second thought and trust that he would land well, surely he could take a chance on her? Trust her?

But she knew that saying she loved him wasn't enough, he needed to see it in action to believe it. Never mind that she had an audience, if she didn't do it now, she'd regret it. This was her one chance to tell him how she really felt and if he rejected her again then she'd take it.

One chance.

So, here she was. Thinking about opening her heart to him, putting herself on the line the way she had with David. Asking. Reaching. Saying the words. The last time had been the biggest mistake of her life. But this was different, because Matthieu was different.

She took a steadying breath. 'Matthieu, I need

you to listen. I was hurt very badly. I didn't want to fall for anyone else. I didn't want to open my heart. I wanted to close myself off, stay apart, be an ice queen. I've always been scared to show my emotions because no one ever seemed to care, but I can't control them with you. I love you so, so much. And I know you're…hesitant, but can we try? At least…' she suddenly felt shy '… I'd like to try.'

But he shook his head, his hand limp in hers. He didn't want her.

*Blue eyes.*

Matthieu's eyes were brown. Weren't they? Maybe she'd been wrong.

'Ahem.' Someone tapped her shoulder.

She put her hand up. 'Please. Wait. Can't you see I'm trying to—?'

'Kiss my staff?'

That voice. *Matthieu.* She looked down at Father Christmas. Two Matthieus? 'What? But…?'

Looking decidedly un-Father Christmassy in his resort salopettes, he helped her to stand up. 'I had to do a few things, then took an urgent call from Justin's mother, so Louis took my place.'

'Oh.' She'd just sworn her love to his best friend.

*Great.*

Her heart thundered against her ribcage. 'How's Justin doing?'

*Not on Christmas Day. Please, not on Christmas Day.*

'He's opened his eyes. He's moving his arms and legs. He has a long way to go, but it looks like he's going to be okay.'

Her heart went into free fall. 'Oh, thank goodness. That's excellent. I'm so relieved.'

'Me, too.' He was laughing, his eyes glittering. 'Now, I want to know why you're kissing my staff in front of the whole resort?'

'I thought it was you. I wanted you to know how I feel.'

'Can I get up now? I'm getting cold,' Louis grumbled and Matthieu helped him stand up. 'Are you okay?'

'I will be when I've watched this.' Louis slapped his friend on the back. 'Go on, mate. You've been a real pain for the last few hours. Don't let her get away. Don't mess this up.'

'I don't intend to.' He took her hands and, in front of the whole community who had gathered round he said, 'Rachel, you said you loved me.'

'Yes. I do. More than anything.'

'You've said it before.'

She smiled, remembering. 'This time I mean it. Really mean it. I *love you*, love you, Matthieu. I didn't want to, but I couldn't help it. Now I want everyone to know. I love you.'

He nodded, his eyes shimmering. 'And I'm an idiot. I think everyone will agree?'

Jeers erupted from the crowd.

'A scared idiot, too. I didn't think much of love, to be honest. It didn't help my mum and it just smashed my heart. So, I did what you did, Rachel. When it came to relationships, I locked those smashed pieces away. But then you came along, and you challenged me in so many ways. You cared for me, hurt for me. And you've started to put those pieces back together.'

Her throat was raw. 'Matthieu—'

'But then I felt so *much* for you I panicked. I thought I could lock everything up again, but I can't.'

Rachel pressed her lips together, holding back a sob. 'We've both been hurt before, Matthieu. It's hard to let ourselves fall into something like this.'

'We get to choose, though. We decide if we want to let someone in. And I choose you, Rachel Tait.'

She couldn't believe it. He hadn't fought for her, for them, last night. But even if he had she wouldn't have wanted to hear it. She'd set her mind on leaving.

But now he was saying these words. Words she'd never thought she'd hear from anyone. She could see the love and the trust in his eyes. 'I choose you, too.'

He reached into his pocket and pulled out a little box. 'I have a gift for you. To show you that I want you to have everything you ever wanted.

To show you how much I care…no…how much I love you, Rachel, and want to keep on loving you.'

'Is it…? No.' She shook her head. A proposal was too soon. She wasn't sure she even wanted a wedding after her last disastrous attempt. 'What…?'

He pushed the box closer. 'Open it. I think you'll understand.'

Heart thundering, she took the box and opened it. Inside, a pair of crystal and silver ballet shoe earrings twinkled and sparkled. She gasped, understanding exactly. He couldn't give her her childhood dream, but he could give her the next best thing.

Her throat felt tight, but her chest felt blown wide open. He listened. He saw her. He loved her. 'Oh, Matthieu, they're beautiful.'

'Like you.' He kissed her cheek. 'I want you to know I hold your dreams and will help you chase them. I believe in you and I want to hold your heart and your hand for ever.'

'Oh, Matthieu.' The last vestiges of fear melted away. 'Thank you.'

'And I know you were badly let down when you should have been happiest. I want you to know, I will never let you down.'

Her wedding day? 'It's too early to talk about things like that.'

'My love will last for ever, Rachel. I'll wait

until you're ready.' He closed his hand over hers. 'I promise with all my heart.'

'Thank you. Thank you so much. But I don't have anything to give you.'

'I can think of a few things.' He laughed and drew her closer. 'How about coming over to my place and having our own Christmas celebration. Just the two of us?'

'Definitely.' She leaned in, trying to shut out all the cheers and applause. He chose her. She let the words settle in her heart. This amazing man chose *her*.

Then he kissed her, and the rest of the world melted away…and she knew it would be the first of many happy Christmases together.

# EPILOGUE

*One year later...*

'THIS HAS BEEN the best Christmas ever.' Matthieu wrapped Rachel in a hug and kissed her neck. The show had gone well, no one had fallen this time, the guests were happy, the evening was just theirs to enjoy.

She looked out of the lodge window and sighed, knowing she'd never get tired of this view. Then leaned into her husband, definitely never getting tired of that view either. She twisted her shiny new wedding ring round her finger and hugged him close. In the end she hadn't wanted to wait and their wedding last month had been a simple ceremony with no aisle, no parents and no surprises. 'Best year ever.'

*And going to get better...*

He squeezed her gently. 'Okay. Sit down, we've done all the hard work. It's time to relax.'

'Wait—' She felt him slip away from her and heard the pop of a champagne bottle cork.

*Aargh. Too late.* 'Um...can I have hot chocolate instead?'

'No bubbles?' Frowning, he poured out a glass for one, then put a pan on the stovetop and poured milk into it, discreetly adding the secret ingredients that he still refused to divulge.

'Not today, thanks.'

*Not for nine months, actually...*

'You feeling okay?' His smile turned into a concerned frown.

'I'm—'

'Fine?' He laughed. Then he peered at her. 'Not fine? What's wrong, *chérie*?'

She was more than fine. Damned fine. The finest she'd ever felt in her whole life. She tried to hide her excitement but couldn't. 'I have a present for you.'

'But you gave me my gifts this morning.'

'One more.' She reached to the back of their little Christmas tree and pulled out a box she'd hidden. 'Happy Christmas, darling.'

He looked at her, eyes narrowing. 'But? What—?'

'Open it.' Her heart was thumping.

He tore the wrapping paper off and opened the box, pulling out the tiniest pair of ski boots ever made. 'What's this? These are baby size.'

Her heart swelled. 'We're going to need them.'

'What?' His eyes shone as reality dawned and he pressed his palm to her non-bump. 'Wow. A baby? A dad? Me?'

'Yes, Matthieu. And you'll be amazing at it.'

He kissed her long and hard. 'Our baby is going

to have the best parents in the world. I love you, Rachel Tait.'

After their dysfunctional childhoods they deserved a proper family. One filled with love and not fear. With understanding, not one-upmanship. With an abundance of health and happiness.

She put her hand over his, over her stomach. 'I love you, too. Or should it be, I love you two?'

He nuzzled her hair. 'Really, truly the best Christmas ever.'

And only going to get better.

Just the three of them and a whole lot of love.

\* \* \* \* \*

*If you enjoyed this story, check out these other great reads from Louisa George*

Nurse's One-Night Baby Surprise
The Princess's Christmas Baby
A Nurse to Heal His Heart
A Puppy and a Christmas Proposal

*All available now!*